SLOANE SISTERS

S0-BCL-882

SLOANE SISTERS

A NOVEL BY ANNA CAREY

HARPER TEEN
An Imprint of HarperCollins*Publishers*

HarperTeen is an imprint of HarperCollins Publishers.

Sloane Sisters
Copyright © 2009 by Alloy Entertainment
All rights reserved. Printed in the United States of America.
No part of this book may be used or reproduced in any manner whatsoever
without written permission except in the case of brief quotations embodied
in critical articles and reviews. For information address HarperCollins Children's
Books, a division of HarperCollins Publishers,
1350 Avenue of the Americas, New York, NY 10019.
www.harperteen.com

alloy**entertainment**
Produced by Alloy Entertainment
151 West 26th Street, New York, NY 10001

Library of Congress catalog card number: 2008940113

ISBN 978-0-06-117576-3

Design by Andrea C. Uva

09   10   11   12   13   CG/RRDH   10   9   8   7   6   5   4   3   2   1

❖

First Edition

For the sisters I've found in friends

SLOANE
SISTERS

PROLOGUE

Once upon a time there lived four beautiful, fabulous sisters. Except they aren't sisters yet. And that once upon a time? Well, it's now.

There are a lot of stories about girls in New York City, but nothing beats a modern fairy tale. And no place is more magical than Manhattan, with its glittering skyscrapers, stately town houses, and glamorous residents.

Our story begins with Cate and Andie. Their mom died when they were both pretty young. Sounds like the start of a Disney movie, right? Wrong. Cate thinks her past tragedy excuses her present diva attitude. As for Andie, all she wants is to steal the spotlight from her picture-perfect older sister. If only she had a fairy godmother—er, godsister—to help her figure out how. . . .

Across the pond, Stella's as beautiful and breezy—not to mention social—as a butterfly. Her younger sister Lola? Not so much. But maybe a change of scenery can transform this cheeky caterpillar into a charming beauty. After all, isn't metamorphosis the most timeless theme of all?

So sit back and enjoy this little bedtime story. And don't think you know how it'll all come to a close.

Not all fairy tales have happy endings. . . .

THERE'S NO PLACE LIKE HOME

Stella Childs watched, annoyed, as her twelve-year-old sister Lola held her Burberry cat carrier steady on the black leather seat and peered inside.

"Don't be scared, Heath Bar," Lola cooed. "We're here! New York Sit-aaaay!"

A few whiskers poked out the front of the mesh grate and the giant orange cat mewed. Stella rolled her eyes and turned back toward the window.

"Stella, darling, you all right?" Emma Childs glanced across the limo at her oldest daughter, who was sitting on the other side of the cat carrier, tracing a finger over a red line in the Burberry plaid.

"Fine." *Just fine.* Stella rolled down the tinted window and let the warm wind whip through her shoulder-length blond curls. Times Square flew past outside, with its towering walls of garish billboards. A six-story-high Rolex watch showed the time: 4:07. Which meant it was a little after nine o'clock in London. Robin Lawrence was having a party at his flat in South

Kensington, just like he did every year the Friday before school started. He had huge dark brown eyes and wild black hair that looked like it was cut with a machete. He was adorable. Stella should have been there.

Emma kept her green eyes on Stella and unbuttoned the top of her beige cropped trench coat. "I'm looking forward to spending the weekend together, getting settled before you girls start school. I missed you both so much this summer."

Stella and Lola had spent the summer in Tuscany with their grandmother, who had moved there ten years ago to grow organic grapes and make her own vinegarlike wine. But anything was better than being stuck in London, where the tabloids were cataloging every detail of their parents' recent divorce.

"Mum, are you going to be on the Ralph Lauren billboards?" Lola asked excitedly, staring up at an advertisement for Calvin Klein tighty-whiteys.

"I assume," Emma replied. "But we haven't started shooting yet, so not for a while."

Stella rolled her eyes. Emma, as British as cricket, tea, and crumpets, was now the face of the most American label on the planet. Soon she'd be eating corn dogs and throwing barbecues for the Fourth of July.

"Will you sit front row at their show at Fashion Week?" Lola continued excitedly.

"Probably." Emma just smiled.

"When you do, make sure you thank Ralph for ruining my life," Stella muttered, keeping her eyes on the mustard yellow cab speeding next to them. The little boy in the back seat had his thumb lodged up his nose.

"I know this is hard for you, Stella, but New York will be good for us. Winston is so excited to have you here, too," her mom said softly. "I'm glad you'll finally have a proper introduction."

Stella curled her toes in her Juicy espadrilles. There was that name again—*Winston.* The first time Stella heard about Winston was in the spring, after Emma got back from signing the Ralph Lauren contract in New York. Stella and Lola had been walking with their mom in Kensington Gardens, watching the miniature sailboats cut across Round Pond, when Emma dropped the news. Stella had only processed a few words—*deep connection, New York, magical, banker, two daughters*—but it had been enough to know her mum had a boyfriend. And she didn't want to think about Emma having a "deep connection" with anyone.

Five months later, it was clear that Winston wasn't going to disappear—but Stella intended to stay as far away from him as possible. After all, New York was a city of eight million people. How hard could it be?

Her mother kept her eyes on her older daughter as she finger-combed Lola's wind-knotted waves. "I know you're angry with me right now," she said as the limo wove through Central Park, where groups of teenage girls were sprawled on beach blankets, enjoying their lazy Friday afternoons. "But moving here is the right thing for all of us. I couldn't keep you in London a second longer. This job wasn't just a good opportunity for me—it's going to be good for all of us. It's just—" Her mom's voice cracked.

Stella waited for her to go on, to mention her dad and the affair that had brought them to New York, but she didn't.

Lola shot Stella a why-do-you-have-to-be-such-a-horrid-person look, but Stella just sneered back. She wasn't horrid, she was honest.

It was true that London had been awful this past year, but Stella was supposed to go to the Millshire Preparatory School this fall, the most elite school in London. She had already gone shopping with her best friends Pippa and Bridget for outfits for the entire first semester. But now she'd be attending Ashton Prep, an *all-girl* school where they wore *uniforms* every day. It was such a waste to leave London now, with a new wardrobe that would only get to come out and play on the weekends.

Stella bit a cuticle. She hated New York City. She hated that she had to leave her friends, her school, her clothes, her *life* behind. But more than anything, she hated Cloud McClean, that unitard-wearing, pop-singing *twit* who had stolen her father, Duke Theodore "Toddy" Childs, from her mom—from all of them.

After she'd found out that her dad was cheating with the Britney Spears of the U.K., she hadn't wanted to talk about it or think about it. Even now, Pippa and Bridget were the only two people outside her family who knew *why* her parents had divorced.

"Sorry, Mum," Stella finally said, so quietly she doubted Emma could hear. Her mom pressed her finger to her temple and sighed. Even when Emma was nervous or upset, she still looked beautiful. Her light blond hair fell just to her shoulders, and her weekly facials gave her skin a permanent glow.

"Look!" Lola shouted.

The limo sped north up a wide avenue, and Stella watched the shops pass one by one—Armani, Versace, Donna Karan, Chloé—feeling like she'd spotted a few old friends. Stella slid into the middle seat to look over Lola's shoulder. A girl with enormous black Gucci sunglasses waltzed out of Donna Karan, clutching a handful of shopping bags from Searle and Prada.

After a few more blocks, they turned down a tree-lined street and pulled over in front of a Victorian that was five stories tall and covered with shiny green ivy. Protruding from one side of it was a brick tower, making it look like a castle. There was a short wrought iron fence out front and a glossy black door with a wide half-moon window above it.

"This is it," Emma told the girls, studying their faces.

"Bloody hell," Stella breathed, staring at the massive brick building.

"Stella, language," her mom said gently.

"It's brilliant!" Lola cried, pushing out the door, cat carrier in hand. "Look, Heath Bar!" Her skinny arms strained to lift up the canvas bag so the twenty-pound cat could get a better view. "It's practically a castle!"

Heath Bar pushed his pink nose against the mesh and mewed.

"This is . . . our new house?" Stella asked, sliding across the slick seat and stepping out. She loved her town house in West London, a three-story beige building with two pillars on either side of the red front door. But *this* was grand, a house fit for a princess—a newly transplanted Upper East Side princess.

"Mum?" Stella peered into the car. Emma was sitting with her hands on her lap, her face a little pale. "Mum?"

"Right," Emma said, finally following them onto the sidewalk. The driver, a muscular redheaded man, walked around to the back of the limo and opened the trunk. Emma brought her fingers to the platinum chain around her neck and played with it nervously. "I have something to tell you."

Lola spun around and set the carrier on the sidewalk. Heath Bar mewed again. "Do we each get our own floor?" she asked, her green eyes wide.

"No . . ." Emma answered slowly, resting her hands on the front of her dark wash A.P.C. jeans. "It was difficult to find a place over the summer, so I thought we could try something a little more . . . *temporary.*"

"This is brilliant, mum, really." Stella wondered if it had a garden out back or one of those funny lap pools where you could swim forever and always stay in the same place. Maybe living here wouldn't be so bad after all.

The driver set the four Louis Vuitton suitcases on the sidewalk. Stella grabbed the handle of one of the smaller ones, ready to break down the door.

"Stella . . ." Her mom rested a hand on her shoulder to stop her. "This is Winston's town house. We're going to be staying with him for a while, here, with his daughters."

"*What*?" Stella spun around.

Lola pressed her hands to her freckled cheeks.

"It's a trial period," Emma continued. "We're going to take it day by day and see how we all get along. This way you can start Ashton Prep with the girls on Monday." Stella squeezed the suitcase handle tight, the leather sticky against her skin. "I think you'll like them, Stella. They're quite lovely."

Stella looked back at the house, her head spinning. There was a small gold plaque above the mailbox, engraved with the word SLOANE. The black metal box was filled with mail—the *Sloanes'* mail. She peered inside the front window. The foyer was all white marble, with a massive staircase and an ornate silk chair that looked like it had been stolen from Versailles. It was the Sloanes' foyer—their staircase, their chair. In one of the top windows a girl peered out from behind the curtain.

The house suddenly didn't seem *that* incredible.

Lola clapped her hands together quickly in front of her face, the way she always did when she was excited. It was beyond annoying, but right now Lola's spastic movements were the least of Stella's problems.

A man opened the door and walked out onto the stone steps. "Emma!" he called. He was in his late forties, with salt-and-pepper hair and a tanned, chiseled face. He wore a crisp blue button-down shirt and burgundy penny loafers.

"You must be Stella," Winston said, reaching out his hand. Stella kept her arms firmly at her sides. No way. There was absolutely no way she was going shake this man's hand, let alone live in his home.

She turned to step back inside the limo, but it was already pulling away from the curb. *It isn't too late,* she thought as it stopped at the red light at the end of the block. She could make a run for it. The driver would take her to JFK and she'd get on the next plane back to Heathrow. She'd stroll in the gate of Millshire in her strappy blue sailor dress, flanked by Pippa and Bridget, and they'd have another fabulous year.

But then the light turned green, and the limo disappeared around the corner.

Stella looked back at her mom's worried face, at Winston's overtanned-from-a-season-in-the-Hámptons nose, at Lola's wide green eyes, and then back at the Sloanes' house. The girl had disappeared from the window.

She let go of her Louis Vuitton carryall and it fell to the sidewalk with a thud. Winston took her limp hand in his and shook it up and down for a good ten seconds, smiling like he was a little dim.

Welcome home!

MIRROR, MIRROR, ON THE WALL, WHO'S THE FAIREST OF THEM ALL?

Cate Sloane tucked her dark brown hair behind her ears and studied herself in the white-framed full-length mirror. Her navy Tory Burch shift with the silver logo button near the collar whispered, *Most Likely to Succeed.*

Unfortunately, she needed something that screamed, *Will Attack if Provoked.*

She threw a kelly green cashmere cardigan over her shoulders, but it made her feel like she was celebrating St. Patrick's Day five months too late. It wasn't right. Nothing was right anymore. Any second she'd be living with Emma's daughters—Stella and Lulu. *Lulu!* She'd already suffered through twelve of her fourteen years with Andie—suck-up, wannabe Andie, so short she could be mistaken for a refugee from Munchkinland. Wasn't that enough?

She crossed the room to the window, pulling off the sweater and tossing it on the floor. Her floral Anthropologie duvet was folded three times at the edge of her bed, and all six pillows were resting two by two on the white iron headboard, the carnation pink neck roll centered in front. The magazines on her shabby-chic white nightstand were fanned out like in a doctor's office, and the ornate white picture frames on the wall behind her bed hung in a perfect line. Everything was perfect . . . except for the fact that her town house was about to be invaded by British losers with bad avant-garde fashion and even worse teeth.

Cate's iPhone buzzed. She riffled through the black-and-white Balenciaga bag sitting on her desk chair.

BLYTHE: TXT WHEN EVIL STEPSISTERS ARRIVE. NEED 2 HEAR EVERYTHING.

For the first time all day, Cate smiled. Blythe Finley was a good friend, the best Cate had ever had. She was the one who'd brought Cate peanut butter–fudge Tasti D-Lite when she had her tonsils out; the one who'd nominated Cate for not one, not two, but three eighth-grade superlatives: Most Stylish, Best Hair, and an all-new category, Fiercest. And Blythe was the one who'd suggested Cate be the president of the Chi Beta Phis.

The Chi Beta Phis were the most popular girls at Ashton Prep. Cate and Blythe, along with their best friend Priya Singh, had founded the "sorority" four years ago after Veena, Priya's older sister, told them about the secret sororities at Yale. They'd each used a letter for their name: Chi for Cate, Beta for Blythe, and Phi for Priya. Sophie Sachs was the newest member—they'd let her in in sixth grade, after she transferred to Ashton Prep from Donalty. Cate had insisted they not add a fourth letter for

Sophie, because the sorority's name would be awkwardly long, and Sigma was kind of an ugly word anyway. Sophie, wanting to get involved, had made up a complicated secret handshake that involved pinching the other person's butt. But it was so silly they'd stopped doing it after two weeks.

The intercom crackled and Winston's voice filled the room. "Cate . . ." he said in a deep, commanding voice, like he was the dad in some lame TV sitcom. "They're here. . . ."

Cate leaned over her petal pink desk and looked out the window. Her dad was acting like she'd *asked* for a new family. She'd asked him for a lot of things—a private roof deck off her room, a red BMW convertible on her sixteenth birthday, a summerhouse in Nice—but she'd definitely never asked for a new family. But there, standing in front of her house, were Emma and two blond girls. Cate could only see the tops of their heads.

She felt for the sapphire ring on her finger and rubbed the flat blue stone with the pad of her thumb. It was times like these that she missed her mom the most. Since she died, Cate tried to wear something of hers every day just to feel like she was there. Yes, it had been six years, but it still felt too soon. Like someone had pushed the fast-forward button on her life.

The intercom crackled again. "Cate . . . ?" Her dad's voice trailed off.

Cate got up and pushed a button on the beige plastic unit near the door. "*I'm. Coming,*" she growled through clenched teeth. Winston didn't respond.

She walked into her closet and pulled on her go-to outfit: dark-wash skinny J Brand jeans, black ballet flats, and a Nanette

Lepore silk leopard-print tank. She threaded a gold leaf earring through each ear and took a deep breath. Whoever these girls were, and however horrifyingly bad their dental hygiene, she was living with them now. Her strategy would be to do what she did best: stay on top—no matter what.

When she got down to the wide mahogany staircase her heart sped up. She took a few steps and peered over the banister. Emma was standing next to the hall closet, clutching Winston's hand and smiling relentlessly, the way Ms. Elsa Kelley, Cate's trying-way-too-hard earth science teacher did right after she got her teeth bleached. The afternoon light flooded in from the half-moon window over the door, making the white marble foyer look too bright and cheerful.

Cate glided down the stairs, keeping her head held up high. In her leopard-print shirt she felt like a wild animal surveying its territory. *This is* my *house,* she thought, pulling her shoulders back. *My turf.* She stopped on the final step, a few inches above everyone else. The two blond girls were standing across from Winston and Emma, in front of the mahogany credenza. Four Louis Vuitton suitcases sat in a row beside them.

"Hi!" Emma called loudly, letting go of Winston's hand and hugging Cate tightly—a little too tightly for someone she'd only met a few times before. Emma had been around all summer, which meant Cate had spent the summer avoiding her.

As Emma finally released her, Winston nodded at the two girls and then toward Cate. "This is my Cate," he said proudly. The younger one, a gangly girl with blond hair that looked like it had been washed with pool water, stepped forward. She was holding a Burberry carrier with some sort of . . . *creature*. Cate wrinkled her nose. She *hated* animals. "Cate," Emma said softly, wringing her hands together, "this is Lola."

Right—Lola. Cate stared at the girl. Lola—which wasn't a much better name than Lulu—was tall and bony and awkward. She looked like a dying giraffe. A dying giraffe who was wearing tapered jeans that were an inch too short. Cate's stomach churned miserably. The last thing she needed was another loser sister to avoid in public.

"Hi," Cate said flatly, crossing her arms over her chest. She flicked her eyes over the girl's lanky frame and held her gaze on her bare ankles just a few seconds too long.

"Stella, luv," Emma coaxed. "Come here." Stella walked across the foyer to the staircase and stood next to Winston. He was scratching his neck, waiting to see what would happen next.

Cate pursed her lips and coolly surveyed the girl from head to toe. Stella had loose blond curls that just hit her shoulders and huge eyes the color of martini olives. She was wearing a red sleeveless Diane von Furstenberg dress with black piping around the neckline. Over her shoulder was a gray Marc Jacobs Mercer East/West tote—the same exact one Cate had looked at in Bergdorf's last week.

The girls stood in silence for a moment. Winston coughed loudly and glanced at Emma, who was still wringing her hands, her lips pressed together in a straight line. Then Cate stepped down from the last step, her feet barely making a sound on the marble. She looked Stella right in the eye and slowly smiled.

"Hey," she said softly. If her outfit was any indication, Stella was . . . normal. Someone Cate *could* be seen in public with. She could even imagine them walking down the hall at Ashton Prep together. Shopping in Soho together. Lying out in Sheep Meadow, talking about the Marc Jacobs spring collection.

Stella reached out and touched the thick strap of Cate's silk tank.

"I love your top," Stella said in a lilting British accent. "Nanette Lepore's brill. And those earrings. They're smart."

Cate's lips curled into a smile. "I love your bag!" she couldn't help gushing. "It's incredible." She gently touched the putty-colored leather.

"My mum got it for me. It was a present from one of her clients." Stella eyed the bag and shrugged.

Cate stared at Emma in disbelief. Swag? From clients? She'd never even thought of that. Maybe she could forgive Emma for dating her father, for moving to New York, for Lola, or Lulu, or whatever-her-name-was with the frizzy hair and bad tapered jeans. If this meant an unlimited supply of designer handbags, yes, she could definitely forgive her.

Winston turned and kissed Emma on the forehead. He wrapped an arm around her shoulder.

"Great shoes." Cate pointed to Stella's red espadrilles. "Juicy?"

Stella nodded and slipped the right shoe off her foot. She nudged it forward with her tiny toes, which were painted with a French pedicure. Cate carefully slipped her foot out of her black ballet flat and into the sandal.

Cate held her breath. Stella held hers. As it had for Cinderella, everything depended on the shoe's fit.

Cate pushed her toe to the front and gently pressed down her heel. It was perfect. She clasped Stella's hands and rocked up and down on the balls of her feet, imagining her wardrobe doubling.

"It fits!" Cate cried, and Stella let out a laugh, revealing her dimples.

Stella slipped on Cate's ballet flat and held out her foot, admiring the fit.

"Perfect!" she exclaimed.

You're perfect! Cate almost cried, barely capable of containing her excitement. As soon as she thought it, she knew it was true. If there had been a Shopbop.com for stepsisters, Cate could not have picked out a better one herself.

WISH UPON A STAR . . .
A VERY FAMOUS STAR

Twelve-year-old Andie Sloane walked up Fifth Avenue past the Metropolitan Museum, her cleats clicking on the concrete sidewalk. The museum's stone steps were covered with tourists devouring foot-long hot dogs, arguing over guidebooks, and basking in the late-August afternoon sun. A crowd gathered around the long narrow fountain in front of the museum, watching in horror as a bereted street performer swallowed a whole set of Henckels knives.

Andie stopped at the corner of Eighty-second Street and studied her reflection in the mirrored doors of the Excelsior, an apartment building that looked like a giant Tootsie Roll. She pouted her lips and put one hand on her hip, striking a quick pose. Sure, in her soccer uniform she looked more Nike than Nicole Miller, but she still had all the right moves.

"Girlie, I told you these doors are two-way," a doorman stuffed into an extra-small green uniform said, stepping outside. "You're giving the lobby a show again."

Andie laughed and took off down the street. As of five o'clock today, she'd be sharing her town house with supermodel Emma Childs. She had to *prepare*.

It was Andie's dream to be a high-fashion model. She watched *America's Next Top Model* religiously and took notes on what the judges said. Every night she practiced her poses in the full-length mirror on her closet door: She knew how to do editorial, she knew avant-garde. She pushed herself to be creative and think of outside-the-box poses.

She couldn't look through *Teen Vogue* anymore without throwing the magazine down, annoyed. She was just as good as any of those models. So what if she was four-foot eleven (fine . . . four-foot ten and three-quarters)? That was why she idolized Kate Moss: She wasn't six feet tall, and yet she was one of the most famous models on earth. Andie always asked herself, WWKD (What Would Kate Do)?

But now she could ask, WWED (What Would Emma Do)? And then she could ask Emma herself.

Or her daughters.

Andie stopped in front of her family's five-story brick town house and smiled, imagining herself lying out in the garden with Emma's fashionista daughters. The two mini Emmas would tell her which shade of tan looked best in photographs and help her decide on a go-to outfit for agent meet-and-greets. For once in her life, she wouldn't be spending Friday nights watching TV by herself, listening to the giggles and shouts of Chi Beta Phi's karaoke sleepover upstairs. She would have new sisters, two chances to start over with girls who wouldn't just see her as an annoying hanger-on copykitten.

It hadn't always been that way between her and Cate. They used to be close, when they were little. They'd dress up in their mom's clothes and play Runway, and Cate would rate Andie's silly outfits. Andie was always trying to make Cate laugh, and get a ten. But when their mom passed away, Cate started hanging out with the Chi Beta Phis more and more. Andie tried to be part of Cate's group, to be someone Cate would want not just as a sister but as a friend. She secretly used her sister's MAC makeup and stole Cate's Luckys, buying everything flagged with a colorful YES sticker. She never once made plans on Chi Beta Phi sleepover nights, hoping that if they saw her in the living room watching *The Hills*, they might plop down on the couch beside her. But they never did. Cate would rather have shopped at Kmart for a year than let Andie hang out with her and her friends. Instead, she made fun of her, calling her C.C.—Copy Cate. In the Chi Beta Phis, Cate had three sisters. Apparently she didn't need one more.

Andie was resigned to life in Cate's shadow—she'd even perfected the art of pretending it didn't bother her. But then one day, she and Cate had been eating ice cream on the steps of the Met when a woman in a pantsuit approached and asked Andie if she'd ever thought of modeling. Not Cate—*Andie*. After the woman left, giving Andie her card, Cate had laughed it off. It was just a ploy to hook naïve girls, she said. They'd get you to pay for head shots and totally rip you off. Andie? A *model*?

But if there was anything Andie hated, it was being told what she could and couldn't do. She knew then and there that modeling was her destiny. Forget being like Cate. She'd be *better than* Cate.

Andie opened the front door. The crystal chandelier in the foyer made a tinkling noise. In the kitchen someone laughed. *Emma.* Andie looked at her stopwatch—it was four forty-five, which meant they were early and she was a sweaty, mud-stained mess. Andie couldn't meet Emma's daughters looking like the motocross champion of Nevada.

She gently set her soccer bag by the door and kicked off her dirt-caked cleats. She crept over to the marble staircase, trying to get upstairs to shower before anyone realized she was home.

"Look who's here!" Cate leaned out of the arched kitchen doorway. "Now, don't you look nice?" She smiled tauntingly at Andie's stained soccer uniform.

"Cate . . . no," Andie whispered, pointing to her dirty knees and the pit stains that were soaking her gray T-shirt. She had the perfect outfit laid out on her desk chair upstairs—she just had to get to it.

Emma stepped out from behind Cate and smiled her famous *Vogue*-cover grin. "Andie!" She smoothed Andie's side-swept bangs from her sweaty forehead, then kissed her on each cheek. Even though she'd met Emma more than a few times now, Andie still hadn't gotten over the shock that *Emma Childs* was her dad's girlfriend—that *Emma Childs* looked happy to see her. If she needed a sign that modeling was her destiny, it was that her dad had met Emma in the first place. "Come, there's someone I want you to meet."

Andie reluctantly followed Emma, her fingers tugging at the blond highlight in her bangs. Her dad said she was too young to dye her hair, so she'd dipped a strand in hydrogen peroxide before their trip to Hawaii this summer, then blamed it on the sun.

"Andie Sloane," Emma urged gently, "this is my oldest daughter, Stella Childs. You'll meet Lola in a second—she just ran off to the loo."

Andie looked past her dad to the center island. Stella—blond, curly-haired, tall, Diane von Furstenberg–clad Stella—was leaning on the granite island, popping green grapes into her mouth. The same Stella Childs Andie had read about in an *Allure* article last year, the one who'd said she was considering starting her own clothing line, and mentioned how Paulina Porizkova was like an aunt to her.

"We'll leave you girls to get acquainted," Winston said with a conspiratorial grin, as if it wasn't painfully obvious he assumed that the mere act of him leaving the room would create some sort of love bubble with all the girls. He and Emma walked into the living room and sat down at the round cherry table. He opened two royal blue folders with the Ashton Prep crest on the front and started shuffling through paperwork.

"Hey, Stella." Andie pulled her shoulders back to make herself seem taller and extended her hand.

Stella leveled her eyes at Andie and smiled slightly. "Hey, C.C. Cate's told me *all* about you." She barely touched Andie's hand as she shook it, her eyes resting on the hole in the toe of Andie's right sock.

Andie felt the blood rush to her face. Cate had told Stella *all about her*? She knew what that meant. That she was a loser. A wannabe. That one time Cate had advised Andie to buy slouch socks in every color, swearing eighties fashion was coming back—and she'd done it.

Cate flicked her eyes back to Stella and continued on, as if Andie wasn't there. "The skirt is mandatory, but they're not that strict about how you wear it. I usually roll mine at least three times—they say to the knee, but Catherine McCafferty is the only one who wears it like that, and she also wears *white Reeboks*." The two girls giggled, their laughter tinkling like silverware on crystal.

Andie studied Stella, searching for any sign that she might still have a chance at being friends with her. But Stella's face was hardened in concentration, as though she were creating a mental spreadsheet of every word Cate said. Andie's stomach folded like a paper crane. Forget tanning with her new sisters in the garden—she'd be lucky if Stella didn't try to turn her room into a walk-in closet. Andie stood frozen, gripping the cold granite counter.

"Well, West London's brilliant," Stella told Cate, fingering one of her butter blond curls.

"Is that where Jude Law lives?" Cate rested her elbows on the counter, mesmerized.

"No, no, he's in Primrose. But I saw Kylie Minogue every other day. My mum will have to take us on her next trip back. There's even a street called *Sloane* Street. How perfect? It has all the shops you'd love—Gucci, Tiffany, Chloé, Louis Vuitton."

Cate shrieked and held Stella's dainty, manicured hands in her own. "I want to go *now!*"

"I want to go too," Andie mumbled, but Cate and Stella

ignored her, as though she were only visible to people wearing loser goggles.

"Ow!" a voice behind her cried. Andie turned to see a girl rubbing her shoulder with her hand, staring at the doorway like *it* had just bumped into *her*. She had wavy, dirty blond hair, and her pale face was dusted with freckles. She was tall—almost a foot taller than Andie—and bony. Her shoulders were hunched forward, like she belonged in a bell tower. Even worse, she was clutching a twenty-pound orange tabby, who licked at a spot of what Andie hoped was food on her fur-covered shirt.

Stella and Cate looked at the girl and rolled their eyes, retreating quickly to the garden like she might be contaminated.

"I'm Lola." The tall girl let out a sigh. "And this is my baby, Heathy." She singsonged the word *Heathy*, rocking the giant cat back and forth in her arms.

Andie watched as Lola kissed *Heathy* on the top of his head four times. She tried hard to smile but her face felt stiff, like she'd left a Bliss masque on for three days. Clearly, she and Lola would not be shopping at Barneys together or brunching with Lola's tween model friends. Lola was more cat lady than catwalker.

"I'm Andie," she muttered, staring longingly out the window at Cate and Stella, who had splayed out on the chaise lounge outside.

Lola chewed on her bottom lip and followed Andie's gaze. "I guess you're stuck with the geeky sister," she said, laughing nervously.

Andie let out a small laugh, but she couldn't stop picturing Cate and Stella playing Rock Band in the den together, closing

the French doors when she walked past. She saw them storming the roof in matching bandeau bikinis, kicking her off the
deck so they could sunbathe. She saw them doing yoga in the
garden together, or eating brunch on the terrace together. She
saw herself . . . with Lola . . . sewing Heathy a pair of striped
pajamas.

She watched as Lola pulled a clump of cat hair off her sleeve
and it drifted slowly to the floor. *Yeah*, she thought. *I guess I am.*

"Andie, would you mind giving Lola a proper tour?" Emma
asked, reappearing in the kitchen doorway. She looked back and
forth between the two younger girls hopefully. "Maybe you can
show her to her bedroom?"

Andie smiled thinly as Lola clapped her hands fast in front of
her face, like she was suffering from a severe muscle spasm.

"That'd be brill!" Lola exclaimed. "So far I've only seen the
loo!" She laughed at her own not-funny joke.

Of course I mind, Andie thought. But she wasn't about to tell
Emma Childs, the new face of Ralph Lauren, that her younger
daughter was a pocket protector away from being High Queen
of the Dorks.

"Sounds . . . *great.*" Andie gave Emma an awkward thumbs-up.

She walked into the foyer and up the mahogany staircase,
Lola trailing behind her like an overactive puppy.

"This is the formal dining room," Andie offered at the top of the first flight.

Lola clutched Heath Bar to her chest and stared at the long wooden table. In the center of it sat a cut crystal vase overflowing with white peonies.

"Just be careful—these are from the eighteenth century," Andie said, looking from Heath Bar to the antique-looking wood chairs, all upholstered in ornate brick red damask. "The house was my grandfather's, and my dad kept a lot of his antiques."

Lola took a step back, trying to keep an arm's distance between herself and anything irreplaceable. She had a habit of breaking things, which was why her mum had loved the mod furniture phase that took over London a few years back—lots of plastics and indestructible materials.

Lola glanced in the gilded mirror on the wall, making sure her thick wavy hair concealed the tops of her Dumbo ears, as Stella had dubbed them. She didn't need Stella to reminder her she was an awkward mess, of course. She was quite aware already. But now, it seemed, Cate would be reminding her as well.

Lola eyed Andie's greasy hair, a little relieved. At least *she* didn't seem like she'd go barmy over a new pair of Christian Lou-bou-whatevers.

"We're going to be good mates, I just know it," Lola breathed as they made their way up another wooden staircase. "Stella and I are complete opposites."

"I noticed," Andie replied as they reached the fourth-floor landing. "And this . . ." she continued, opening a door, "is your room." The teal room had a four-poster twin bed covered in a striped duvet, a narrow white dresser, an empty bookcase, a teal armchair, and completely bare walls. Five cardboard boxes were stacked in front of the window, LOLA'S BOOKS scribbled on the side of each.

Lola set Heath Bar down and he slunk over to the armchair, digging his claws into the side of it. "Heathy, no!" she cried, swatting him away.

"My room is just through here," Andie said, ducking into the bathroom that connected the bedrooms. "I'm going to go change."

Lola sat down on her new bed and pulled the giant tabby into her arms, his stomach jiggling like a Jell-O-filled Ziploc. She scanned the room looking for his Kitty Castle, the three-story scratching post she'd bought him for his first birthday. It was missing.

But at least she was right next door to Andie. Maybe Andie would help her unpack her books, and then they'd go to Central

Park and get one of those giant pretzels that everyone in movies seemed to eat when they were in New York. Maybe they'd be in band together—Lola played the viola—and they'd sit tuning their instruments and laughing about the conductor's silly bow tie.

All the maybes swirled through Lola's head as the bathroom door swung open. Out stepped Andie, dressed in the same blue and fuchsia dress Stella had worn to her fourteenth birthday party. Her tiny pedicured feet teetered on wedge heels that triggered Lola's fear of heights. Her hair was smoothed back into a tight bun. Except for a freckle near her lip, she looked almost exactly like Cate.

All Lola could think was, *They're multiplying.*

Lola looked around the room warily, afraid another label-obsessed, Marc Jacobs–clad robot would emerge from her closet, ready to flatiron her hair and torch her Gap wardrobe. She watched as Andie gazed at her reflection in the bathroom mirror.

"What?" Andie asked, noticing Lola's stare. "Is the eye shadow too much? The girl at Sephora told me gold was in."

"No . . ." Lola mumbled. "It's . . . pretty." With big liquid brown eyes and a tiny button nose, Andie belonged in an issue of *CosmoGIRL!*, not playing Pachelbel's Canon in some dorky orchestra.

Lola hugged Heath Bar to her chest so tightly he let out a loud mew.

"So, you can put all of your stuff in these two drawers," Andie said, pointing to the cabinet under the sink. "And you can totally borrow my hair dryer." Andie leaned against the door frame, eyeing Lola's frizzy hair.

"I was thinking," Lola said softly, looking around the bare room. "Would you want to go to Times Square with me?"

Andie laughed, but stopped suddenly when she realized Lola was serious. "Lola," she said, enunciating her words like Lola was a toddler, "that place is the armpit of the city. Only tourists go." Andie's face was scrunched in disgust, like Lola had just picked a scab in front of her.

Lola knew that face. It was the same one Cate had given her in the foyer. The same one Stella gave her every time she passed her in the halls of Sherwood Academy. The face that said, *Um . . . no thanks.*

"I just thought . . ." Lola stuttered. She felt the airplane food churning in her stomach.

"Besides," Andie interrupted. "I have to . . . clean my room." And with that, she disappeared through the bathroom and was gone.

Lola set Heath Bar down on the floor and pulled her long legs into her chest. New York was going to be just like London, where she never had the right clothes, or the right hair. But at least in London she'd had her best mate, Abby. They'd sat in the back of English and made fun of Mr. Porter's arm fat, which flapped back and forth as he wrote on the board.

Lola dug her laptop out of her suitcase and signed onto IM. She scanned her buddy list, but it was after ten in London. Abby wasn't online.

Then her eyes fell on a familiar screen name: Striker15. She did have *one* mate in New York.

Kyle Lewis.

He had lived next door to her in London for three years while his father was teaching at Oxford. They had become buddies, sliding down Kyle's den stairs in their sleeping bags, making mud soup in Regent's Park, loading up their buckets with dirt, sticks, and tulips. She hadn't seen him since she was ten, more than two years ago, but they'd started talking online this summer when she found out she was moving. He'd told her about New York: how she had to make sure to look left, not right, before crossing the street, how her savings—all one hundred and six quid—was going to double (*Ur gonna be rich!!! $$$*, he'd written). He'd even promised to take her to Madame Tussauds if she ever felt home-sick—he'd said it was just as weird as the one in London.

LOLABEAN: I'M HERE! NYC!
STRIKER15: HEY! HOW'S IT GOING SO FAR!
LOLABEAN: SO FAR . . .

She paused and ran her fingers over the keyboard. So far only two out of the five people she lived with liked her—and one of them was her mom. But he didn't need to know that.

LOLABEAN: SO FAR SO GOOD. WANT TO HANG OUT
AFTER SCHOOL ON MONDAY?
STRIKER15: SURE, I CAN MEET U AFTER BAND PRACTICE.

Lola laughed, imagining Kyle with his massive baritone horn case. He was so skinny his mum had bought him a little trolley to wheel it on.

If Lola was uncool, then Kyle was a super geek. He wore thick glasses and had messy Harry Potter hair, a lanky body, and crooked teeth. In fourth grade he'd memorized all the constellations and had made Lola sit with him in the park for an hour while he found each one in the night sky.

Lola breathed a sigh of relief. She and Kyle would hang out on Monday and keep on about missing Christmas crackers and Cadbury Twirl chocolate bars. He'd show her Times Square, even if it *was* the armpit of the city. And they'd drag that silly baritone horn around together, not caring if it was cool or not.

Lola couldn't wait.

EVERY PRINCESS HAS A PEA

Saturday afternoon, Stella and Cate strolled up Madison Avenue, their arms laden with shopping bags. Cate had taken Stella to a sample sale at the Peninsula Hotel and picked a dress out for her, insisting it would go perfectly with Stella's coloring. There were only three people Stella trusted with fashion advice: Bridget, Pippa, and her mum. But looking at her strapless turquoise Vivienne Tam dress nestled inside her shopping bag, she knew she could add Cate to that list.

"It really is a beautiful dress," Stella noted.

"I told you!" Cate singsonged, swinging her Hermès bag in the air.

After the sample sale, Cate and Stella had stopped in all of Stella's favorite shops: Dolce & Gabbana, Donna Karan, Coach. Then they'd lunched at La Goulue. Stella wanted to hate New York, she really did, but it was nearly impossible when Cate Sloane, connoisseur of fine food and clothing, was her personal tour guide.

Cate squeezed Stella's arm. "It's so Zac-Posen-goes-to-Beijing," she added approvingly.

A group of sixth-grade girls zoomed past on their Razor scooters. A girl in an Ashton Prep tee stared intently at Cate and Stella, almost crashing into a parked Audi.

Stella flipped her blond curls over her shoulder, buzzing from the attention. She could hardly wait to walk into her new school arm in arm with Cate. They'd spend all of English drawing pictures of Jane Eyre in Temperley dresses. They'd plan their shopping route in the cafeteria over Waldorf salads. Most of all, they'd dominate the ninth grade. They wouldn't just be the best BFF pairing Ashton Prep had ever seen, because they were more than that. They were practically sisters. What could be better?

They turned down Eighty-second Street, the humid August air making the city feel like one massive sauna. Cate pushed into the air-conditioned house and started up the staircase.

"So what are we doing tonight?" Stella asked, following Cate into her bedroom.

"My friends are sleeping over." Cate dropped her shopping bags in a heap on the floor. Tonight was Chi Beta Phi's first sleepover of the year, and as sorority chair and all-around most popular girl, Cate had to tackle the most pressing issues: accessories for the first day of school, assessment of their current schedule, and strategies for keeping their lunch table by the window just that—*theirs*.

"Brilliant—what are they like?" Stella followed her into her bathroom, hovering in the doorway.

"Well," Cate said proudly, digging through her Kate Spade

makeup bag, "there's four of us. Blythe, Priya, and I have been friends since third grade, Sophie since sixth. We're kind of like . . . a sorority. Our name is Chi Beta Phi, and we have rules. We don't let just anyone in. And I'm pretty much in charge," Cate went on, swiping Clinique mascara on her already long, already dark lashes. "We're supposed to vote for the position each new school year, but I was voted in three years ago and nobody has ever asked for a revote. It's just natural that I would be president—Priya is really funny but too easygoing, and Blythe is pretty and popular but always needs someone telling her what to do. And Sophie is just . . . Sophie is fourteen going on ten, she's so immature." Cate pushed past Stella and out the bathroom door. She pulled Randolph, her stuffed bear, into her lap. "I love those girls, but honestly, they'd be lost without me."

"So what does it mean to be 'in charge'?" Stella furrowed her brows.

Cate looked at Stella's curious face and grinned—she loved a rapt audience. "Well, I hold the first sleepover of the year. And it's always the most important—we catch up and make plans for September. I also decide where we go and what we do, I get to say who's in and who's not, and I know everyone's secrets," Cate said smugly, smoothing down Randolph's ears. "That's not an official rule or anything, it just seems like everyone comes to me when they have problems." She shrugged nonchalantly, as if to say, *Being charitable and understanding comes naturally to me.*

Stella stared out the window at the gray town house across the street, its curtains drawn. Her mates in London didn't have any rules. Bridget and Pippa always wanted her to decide where they were going for brunch, and took her fashion advice very seriously, but Stella wasn't "the sorority leader" or anything like that. She just had good taste.

And wasn't afraid to share it.

Cate's "sorority" sounded a little like a cult. She pictured them drinking goat's blood and tattooing Phi Beta Chi into each other's arms with a Bic pen.

"It's a lot of pressure," Cate continued, smoothing down her glossy dark brown hair. "But the secrets are little things—like Blythe's. She's a serious spray tan addict. If there were a rehab clinic for spray tanners, I'd have an intervention and send her there. She'll disappear for a whole weekend and she'll tell Priya and Sophie that she's in Cabo, then she'll go spray tanning three days in a row." Cate giggled, the words spilling out of her mouth. "And Blythe wears a 'Little Lady' training bra. Because she doesn't have boobs yet."

Stella's eyes widened. "No way—even Lola doesn't wear those anymore!" She erupted in a fit of giggles.

"I know. And Priya tells everyone she goes to sleepaway camp in the Adirondacks, but her parents have been sending her to science camp for the last three years, where she's gotten obsessed with dissecting things. Seriously, Lola'd better keep an eye on Reese's Pieces." Cate paused, wondering if she'd said too much. But who was Stella going to tell, her loser sister? Besides, she loved a rapt audience. Every time she spoke, she imagined herself up onstage, delivering the lines to a theater full of enamored fans. This was better than when she'd played Nellie in *South Pacific*.

"Sophie's secret is the funniest," Cate went on. "She still plays with Barbies."

"No!" Stella gasped.

Cate raised her hand up as if she were being sworn in at court. "She has a whole collection of them—she keeps them under her bathroom sink. She says she never plays with them, but every time I go over there they're in different outfits." Cate cackled, remembering the last time she'd looked under Sophie's sink. One Barbie had her hair in a French braid and was wearing a neon green wet suit.

Cate eyed Stella, her perfect blond ringlets swinging as she threw back her head and laughed. Cate loved the Chi Beta Phis, but Stella was different. Stella would never buy Barbies or cover up a spray tan streak with a giant Band-Aid. It was nice to finally have . . . an equal.

The deck was lit by tiki torches. Chenille blankets were draped over the padded teak couch and the big chaise lounges, and citrus-scented candles sat on the small side tables, making the warm night air smell like lemonade. There were bowls of each girl's favorite snack: Terra Chips for Priya, apple-and-brie sandwiches for Blythe, and gummi bears for Sophie. Mojito and cosmo mocktails sat on the coffee table in pink polka-dotted martini glasses.

Tasteful and elegant, but it doesn't seem like I tried too hard, Cate thought.

She had been waiting for tonight all summer: the night she'd get to hear the full story of how Blythe met Jake Gyllenhaal in Mykonos, the night they'd finally steal Priya back from her camp bestie—some French girl named Audrey who had tried to convince her to wear power-washed denim—and the night she'd tell them all about Charlie, her first kiss. They'd spent two blissful days together on Kapalua Bay beach in Maui, snorkeling and laying out near the coconut groves, sipping virgin piña coladas. Sophie was going to be so surprised, she'd choke on her retainer.

Cate laid out five sleeping bags in a spiral on the roof deck, then stood back to admire her work. Four of them were perfect pink plaid, with mauve lining that matched Cate's couch. The fifth was Winston's old camping bag from the eighties, a huge battered black thing complete with a hood. Cate cringed. It looked like they had invited a dead body to the sleepover.

Cate pulled her iPhone out of her pocket to text Blythe.

CATE: DO U HAVE AN XTRA SLEEPING BAG 4 STELLA?

Her phone instantly buzzed with a reply.

BLYTHE: IM @ YR DOOR. Y??? IS STELLA COMING???

Cate frowned down at the glossy screen of her phone. Ever since she'd heard Emma's spawn were moving in, she'd complained to her friends nonstop about the injustice. She didn't want to seem like a total schizo, suddenly falling all over her new sister and inviting her to their sleepover.

Just then the intercom next to the door crackled and Winston's voice called out in the warm night air. "Cate—your friends are here." Stella walked to the sliding glass door, tugging it open.

"You should wait here." Cate stopped her. "*I'm* excited you're coming to the sleepover, but I don't know how Priya, Sophie, and Blythe are going to take it. Let me warn them first." She smiled sweetly, then slipped through the door and descended the stairs to greet her guests.

Warn them? *Ohh-kay.* Stella shrugged off the weirdness and dipped her finger into the yellow candle wax. She rolled it in a tiny ball and flicked it off the roof. On a terrace across the street, a man in blue silk shorts smoked a cigar. A car alarm blared in the distance. New York, Stella realized, had its own sound track— even the ambulances sounded different than in London. It would take a while to get to know its smells, sights, and sounds.

Just then, the sliding door opened and Cate emerged, followed by three girls, each clutching a puffy paisley Vera Bradley tote.

A girl with dirty blond hair and gray eyes stopped when she saw Stella. Her skin was so tan it looked like she'd eaten radioactive oranges. Blythe. Stella zeroed in on her boobs, but they looked too big to be contained in a "Little Lady" training bra.

"Blythe," Cate said, "this is Stella." Stella stood and reached out her hand, but Blythe just pressed her lips together into a smug smile.

"Hi." She threw her bag down on the deck and walked over to the couch, where she kicked off her bumblebee yellow flats. Stella glanced at the two other girls, wondering what *that* was about.

Priya had pale brown skin and sleek black hair. When she tilted her head, a silver stud in her nose sparkled. Sophie was shorter, and younger looking. Her nose was a little sunburned and she had light brown hair that looked like it had been straightened with a one-hundred-degree industrial iron.

"This is Priya and Sophie," Cate said. Priya nodded and joined Blythe on the couch, picking up a mocktail. Sophie and Cate settled in between Priya and Blythe, taking the last remaining spots.

Stella dragged over a chaise lounge and sat in front of them. Across from her, Sophie was blatantly staring at Blythe's boobs, which looked like they might pop out of her white strapless Juicy Couture dress. "What's the deal, Jessica Simpson?" she finally asked.

"Funny." Blythe smiled mysteriously. "Let's just say Greece was good to me this summer."

Cate eyed Blythe's chest suspiciously. "Becca Greenleaf grew boobs last summer but it turned out it was just the Victoria's Secret water bra."

"What about my nose ring? No one even noticed," Priya pouted.

"I noticed," Sophie squealed. "I told you at the door!"

"I noticed too," Stella added, but still none of the girls looked at her. She was beginning to suspect that Chi Beta Phi might actually stand for Cold Bratty Prisses.

"I have some news too," Cate said, going over to the table where her MacBook Pro was sitting. She smiled as she sat back down with the laptop. Stella went around to the back of the couch to look over her shoulder.

Cate pulled up iPhoto and clicked through a few pictures of her vacation in Hawaii. "These are pictures from Maui."

She clicked past one of her and Andie next to a palm tree, white plumeria flowers tucked behind their ears. Andie was laughing, and for the first time Stella realized how pretty she was. She had wide, round brown eyes and thick rows of dark lashes. Her cheeks were rosy, and her features were tiny and delicate, like a porcelain doll's.

"And this," Cate cooed, stopping on a picture of her and a tan, rugged-looking boy with a dimpled smile, "is Charlie."

It had been taken on the first day she met him, after they came back from a group diving trip to the Molokini reef. He had sat with her on the top deck after she scraped her ankle against a piece of coral.

"O M to the G!" Sophie screamed, crawling over Priya to get a better look.

"He's really cute." Priya nodded at the picture, hypnotized.

Stella leaned against the back of the couch. The boy was wearing a white T-shirt and had light brown bangs that fell in his face.

"Real fit," she agreed, under her breath.

"Fit?" Sophie asked curiously, turning around.

"He's from Minnesota," Cate continued, reveling in the attention. "He even calls soda 'pop'!" Her voice squeaked with excitement. They had e-mailed a few times over the summer, and Cate had suggested New York as the destination for his next family vacation. The only thing better than telling her girls about Charlie would be introducing them to him.

"Adorable," Blythe proclaimed, as Cate clicked through to another photo of her with Charlie sitting on the lime green surfboard he'd rented from the thatch hut on the beach. She shut the laptop and tucked her legs underneath her.

"We kissed!" she cried, the words tumbling out of her mouth.

"O M *Freaking* G!" Sophie squealed again, grabbing Cate's arm.

Cate stared dreamily up into the starry night sky. "It was after dinner," she said slowly, savoring her friends' jealous looks. "We were sitting on deck chairs by the infinity pool, and he was telling me about the snow in Minnesota and then . . . he just leaned in and kissed me. His lips were so soft, it was like kissing a pillow." Cate took a sip of her virgin cosmo and let out a deep sigh.

Priya fell back against the couch and sighed longingly. "I am so jealous."

Cate smirked. "It'll happen one day," she said condescendingly, looking around at her friends. "For all of you guys."

Stella tugged on a golden ringlet and let out a laugh. "What kind of kiss was it?"

"What do you mean, 'What kind of kiss'?" Blythe asked, turning around to lean over the back of the couch.

Stella straightened up and looked at Priya and Sophie, who were watching her. She shrugged. "The first time I snogged Miles Conway, in sixth grade, I nearly choked on his tongue. He was moving it around all crazy, like this." Stella stuck her tongue out as far as she could and twisted it in circles.

"Ew!" Sophie squealed.

"Snogged?" Priya looked at Cate as if she might be able to translate.

"Sorry—kissed," Stella explained. "I made up different names for each snog with my friends Pippa and Bridget. We called Miles the electric eel, and then this boy Aiden that Pippa snogged, the brick wall."

"Well, my kiss with Charlie wasn't any of those," Cate said loudly, crossing her arms over her chest.

"Wait—what's the 'brick wall'?" Blythe pressed. Sophie and Priya had turned around too, their eyes fixed on Stella.

Stella straightened up. "He just pressed his lips against hers and held them there—he even kept his eyes open!" The girls emitted a chorus of *ew!*s, laughing.

Cate gritted her teeth. This was supposed to be *her* moment at *her* sleepover with *her* friends. Stella was *stealing* it.

"And then there's the great white," Stella whispered, chomping her jaws twice. "All teeth."

"Ouch." Priya winced, giggling.

"I like when they open their mouth just a tiny bit," Stella continued, running her hands along the back of the couch. "That's quite nice."

Blythe, Priya, and Sophie were all turned around, sitting up straight as though Stella were Sergeant Snog, calling them to attention.

"Then there's—"

"It was just a kiss," Cate snapped. "Can we leave it at that?"

"Um . . . okay," Stella said, a little surprised. She shrugged and walked back to the lounge chair. Cate was glaring at her, her mouth twisted like she'd just eaten a whole bag of Sour Patch Kids.

"Great dress," Blythe said, leaning toward Stella and pinching the hem of the skirt. Her face glowed in the soft light of the tiki torches.

"My mum got it from a client." Stella ran her thumb along the neckline of the aqua Betsey Johnson halter dress, satisfied. At the last minute she'd chosen it over her new Vivienne Tam dress, wanting to go with one of her favorites.

"What's it like having a model as a mom?" Sophie asked, obviously impressed.

"You didn't tell me Emma was Emma *Childs*!" Priya nudged Cate. "I had to find out from Blythe."

Cate smiled weakly.

"She's just a regular mum, I guess." Stella shrugged. "It's weirder with my dad—he's a duke." Back home, everyone was obsessed with her parents—they couldn't go anywhere without a flock of paparazzi. Now that she was in New York, she sort of missed the spotlight.

"Wait—so you're like a princess?" Sophie asked, her dark eyes bright. She pulled a chenille throw over her bare legs. On the street below, a driver leaned on his horn.

"Not even close," Cate jumped in, rolling her eyes. "He's a *duke*—she would have to marry a *prince* to be a princess." Stella looked stung, but Cate didn't care. They were dressing up as Disney princesses for Halloween this year, and Cate didn't need any competition for Cinderella. Stella could be Jasmine, fine, but they were already at their queen bee quota: one.

"She's still *kind of* royalty," Sophie said in a small voice, offering Stella a tiny smile. Cate glared at her. Sophie was *way* too nice. When Cate had blacklisted Paige Mortimer for calling Cate stuck-up, Sophie had been the one who cracked first, waving at Paige in gym.

Sophie pulled out her retainer, set it down on the table, and snarfed a handful of gummi bears, ignoring Priya's ew-do-you-have-to? look.

"So why'd you move?" Blythe asked Stella.

Stella shrugged. "London was just so over—New York is really the IT place to live right now." She looked out at the glittering skyline and smiled. "And Mum and Winston and all."

"How long have your parents been divorced?" Blythe pressed.

"Not long," was all Stella said. She wasn't about to tell four strangers about her dad's affair. By Monday, it would end up on *Inside Edition.*

"Mine divorced three years ago." Blythe sighed, sipping a mojito mocktail. "My dad says he won't go near my mom unless she's wearing a straitjacket."

"Sounds like someone's got some issues." Stella laughed. "Well, my dad is brilliant—really. He still loves my mum; they're great mates, actually." Stella wished that were true, but the last time her parents were in a room together, it was to argue over their custody agreement.

Blythe stared into her drink.

Sophie nodded, oblivious. "My parents lived in London for a year when I was a baby, so I'm, like, part British. Now that you're hanging out with us, you can teach me the language. How do you say—"

"There is no language, Sophie," Cate interrupted. "They speak *English.*" And, um, *Now that you're hanging out with us?*

Cate dug her manicured nails into the couch cushion. If she didn't do something soon, the Chi Beta Phis were going to erect a Stella Childs statue and start worshipping it at sunrise.

Cate walked over to the other side of the deck, where the sleeping bags were still laid out. She picked up Winston's black camping bag and rolled it up with several quick twists of her wrist.

"This sleeping bag really doesn't *fit*," she said, leveling her eyes at Stella. She tied the bag up with a tight knot and dropped it onto Stella's lap. Her mojito mocktail splashed onto her gold Tory Burch sandals.

"Is your OCD acting up again?" Blythe laughed, eyeing Cate. "It's not a big deal if they don't all match—we used to use Sophie's old Care Bears sleeping bag."

Stella stood up and shook off her sandals, the sleeping bag tucked under one arm. Blythe was wrong—it *was* a big deal. Stella didn't totally get why, but Cate had gone from BFF to be-yotch faster than pleated pants had gone back out of style. Cate clearly didn't want her here, but Stella wasn't going to let her have the last word.

"It's okay. I'll be more comfortable in my own room anyway," she said, smiling fakely at Cate. "It was nice meeting you all."

She'd rather go into Ashton Prep solo than with some pseudo-sorority psychos. After all, she'd never had to fight to be friends with anybody. If there was a permanent A-list, Stella Childs was always at the top.

With that, she threw the bag over her shoulder and strutted toward the sliding glass doors, not bothering to look back.

TO: Andie Sloane
FROM: Cindy Ng
DATE: Sunday, 5:18 p.m.
SUBJECT: I'm back!

Just got back from Maine and can't wait to see you! And I can't wait for you to see *me*. The braces are off and I got my teeth professionally whitened. They're, like, blinding. I'm practically a supermodel. ☺

Not! But I bet you are. Seriously, are you Emma's prodigy yet? The first petite supermodel?

And how are her daughters? I bet you guys are giving each other pedicures and being fabulous together right this second. I'm jealy.

Anyway, see you tomorrow at school!

Xoxoxoxoxoxo
Cinds

TO: Cindy Ng
FROM: Andie Sloane
DATE: Sunday, 6:24 p.m.
SUBJECT: RE: I'm back!

I can't wait to see you, too, and your fab new smile. No, I am not the world's first under-five-foot supermodel yet. All in time, right?
As for your other question . . .
Stella = Evil Cate Clone
Lola = Loser Cat Lady
Cate = Just as nasty as ever
I wish I were an only child.
We're off to some torturous family dinner. Ugh. See you tomorrow.

—A

UNHAPPILY EVER AFTER

Sunday night, Cate glanced sideways at Stella, stabbing a stiff Carolina shrimp with her fork. Ever since the sleepover, Stella had been acting like a total princess: breezing around the town house like she owned the place, "accidentally" unpacking her clothes in the hall closet designated for *Cate's* shoes, finishing the last eggs Norwegian their chef Greta had cooked *specifically* for Cate.

On top of everything, this morning she'd found Lulu's creature using her velvet couch as a scratching post. Couldn't they build it a doghouse out in the backyard or something?

Across the round table, Winston's arm was wrapped around Emma's shoulder. Cate inhaled, the sharp smell of basil pistou stinging her nose. After dinner she was going to tell her dad that Stella had tried to steal all of her friends. Of course Cate didn't *want* to do it, but someone had to let her dad know he couldn't just throw four girls in a house together and expect them all to play nice.

It had only been one weekend, but the Childses' departure was *long* overdue. Surely the thrill of dating a supermodel would wear off soon, and her dad would move on—and the British Invasion would move out.

Emma smoothed down the lapel of Winston's Etro suit. It was pin-striped, which his guy at Barneys assured him was "slimming," but it just made him look like a preppy mobster.

Just then a cell phone blared techno music so loud Cate half expected people to bust out glow sticks and start raving. At the table next to them, a woman with thinning gray hair looked up from the roasted duck breast she was pretending to eat and stared at the girls disapprovingly.

Winston glanced around the table. "No cell phones, girls. Ordinarily I wouldn't mind, but tonight is our first dinner as a fa—"

Cate cringed. He had stopped himself, but she knew he'd been going to say *family*. She looked at Lola, who was slumped in her chair, poking at her crab cake. Andie was looking for split ends— she hadn't said two words all night. *Right*, Cate thought, *one big happy family*.

Emma threaded her arm through Winston's and squeezed.

"Sorry," Stella said, pulling her iPhone from her blue Lauren Merkin clutch. "It's Bridget—just a minute?"

Stella read the message and giggled, then covered her mouth with her hand. "She's too funny," she whispered to Cate, shooting her a smug smile. "She wants to know if you have a unibrow—she doesn't know anyone who took so long to get their first snog."

Cate bit the end off her shrimp and swallowed hard.

Emma glanced up from her chilled fennel soup. "You all right, girls?" she asked, looking from Cate to Stella. In the soft light of the restaurant, her flawless skin glowed.

"Yes, Mum," Stella said, wrapping her arm around Cate's chair and plastering on a fake grin. "We're *great*."

Emma glanced at Lola, who was now dissecting her crab cake as though it might contain buried treasure. "Lola," she coaxed, playing with the silver chain on her neck, "you're awfully quiet. Are you still feeling jet-lagged?"

"Yes," Lola said, glancing around the table at Cate, Stella, and Andie. "That must be it. . . ." She stuck her fork into the crab cake so that it stood up straight. Behind her, two waiters in crisp white shirts strode past.

"Well, you'll get a proper sleep tonight and be all rested up for school tomorrow."

"Cate, tell them something fun about Ashton," Winston prompted, looking to her for support.

Cate leaned back as a blond guy who was too cute to be just a waiter—clearly a wannabe actor—cleared her shrimp tails. "It's good," she said flatly.

The waiter reached around Lola to grab her plate. Lola leaned back, her napkin sliding off her lap. She reached down to get it and hit her head on the corner of Stella's chair. "Ow!" she cried.

"Are you all right?" her mom asked, resting a hand on Lola's thin leg.

"I'm fine," she grumbled, readjusting her hair so it covered her ears.

Two waiters circled the table, dropping off plates of swordfish à la plancha, rib eye with sautéed porcinis, and pan-seared sea scallops. Winston clinked his fork against his crystal champagne glass.

"Dad," Cate hissed, looking around the crowded restaurant. A couple and their teenage son turned away from their dinner to look at them. The boy, in a navy blazer, stared at Winston, then at the girls. Cate sank a little lower in her burgundy velvet chair.

"Girls, we have an announcement," he said, bringing Emma's hand to his lips and kissing it twice. "I am so glad we're all here, together, in New York. Emma and I spent the summer talking about this and planning this, and now it's finally happened. These last couple days have been incredible."

Cate coughed loudly—*incredible* wasn't *quite* the word she would have used.

Stella sneered at Cate.

Andie rolled her eyes.

And Lola let out a shuddering sigh.

Emma tugged at the chain around her neck and smiled at the girls. "It's lovely that you're all getting along so well. You're already treating each other like family—like sisters."

Cate felt like a fish bone had gotten caught in her throat. Stella was not her sister—not even close. She was a fungus. A bacteria. A leech she needed to have removed. Andie might be annoying, but she was relatively harmless.

Emma unclasped the chain from around her neck and something heavy slid into her palm. "I didn't feel right wearing it until we told you girls." She smiled.

"We're engaged!" Winston blurted out. Emma laughed playfully and opened her hand, revealing a glittery ring with a diamond the size of a gobstopper. It looked like something out of a twenty-five-cent machine—too big to be real.

As Winston slipped it on Emma's finger, Cate felt like she was watching some bad romantic comedy. This wasn't her father. That wasn't Emma's ring. And this definitely wasn't her life.

Cate touched the coral Fendi pashmina around her shoulders—her mother's pashmina. Sometimes it felt like Cate was the only one who remembered her.

"Now, Emma, I have a surprise for you," Winston said. "I spoke with Gloria Rubenstein—that wedding planner you loved. And she said there's an opening at the boathouse in Central Park . . . next Sunday."

"Sunday!" Emma let out a small, surprised laugh.

Cate's stomach lurched, like she was in a cab that had stopped short at a light. She turned to Stella, who was biting her lip so hard it looked like she might draw blood.

"I know it's soon," Winston explained, "but I can't wait a year to marry you—I don't even want to wait a month." A waitress near the door was ignoring her tables, hugging a stainless steel water pitcher to her chest, waiting to hear Emma's response. "What do you think?"

Cate glanced at Lola, who was covering her mouth with her bony hand.

"I think that's the most romantic thing I've ever heard," Emma replied, wiping the tears from her face. The waitress set the steel pitcher down on a table and clapped until the manager, a thin man with an unusually large head, rushed over and whispered something in her ear.

Emma wrapped her thin arms around Winston's side, a tear falling down each cheek. Cate felt like she might cry too.

"Girls," Emma explained, looking around the table, "I know it might seem fast, but we've been thinking about this since we met. We both just sort of knew everything was right."

Stella pushed a bloated scallop around her plate with her fork, annoyed. If Winston and her mum "just knew" something, they certainly hadn't bothered to tell anyone else.

"And now here we all are." Emma looked at Winston, a dreamy expression on her face that Cate wished she could Photoshop off.

Winston matched Emma's expression and Stella had to cough to keep from gagging. "We're hiring a wedding planner, of course, but we'd love for you girls to get involved, too," he said. "Stella, since you're such a fashion guru, why don't you pick out the bridesmaid dresses for you and the girls?"

Cate felt like Winston had thrown his tumbler of ice-cold Pellegrino in her face. *Stella* was the fashion guru?

Emma tucked a golden strand of hair behind her ear. "Andie, maybe you could help me pick out the flowers for the tables, and Lola, you could help decide on the band."

Andie straightened up in her chair and offered Emma a small smile.

Cate rolled her eyes. If Emma Childs had asked Andie to wash the kitchen floor with her tongue, she would have jumped at the opportunity.

"And Cate," Winston added, "you could do a tasting at Greene Street Bakery and pick out the perfect cake for us."

Cate gripped the seat of her chair, digging her manicured nails into the silk fabric. She hated desserts—and had ever since she ate her first chocolate chip cookie. Had her dad totally forgotten? She touched the Fendi pashmina again, a knot creeping up the back of her throat.

"Cate?" Winston prompted.

"That . . . sounds great." Cate tried hard to smile. Lola was chewing nervously on a piece of her hair, and Stella was biting her nail. Andie had dissected her scallop into ten tiny pieces. Nobody was looking at anyone else.

So it was official. Their parents were officially getting married. Stella and Lola Childs were officially residents of the Upper East Side. And Cate's life . . . was officially over.

THE SISTERS GRIMM

At eight on Monday morning, Madison Avenue was already crowded with nannies pushing double-wide strollers and businessmen on their Bluetooths, muttering to themselves like they were insane. Andie followed Stella and Cate down the tree-lined sidewalk. She stared at the doughy doorman at the Excelsior, then at a parked yellow Volkswagen bug, then at a sweaty old man running shirtless down Eighty-ninth Street—anywhere except at Lola. Winston had asked Andie to walk Lola to school, but he hadn't said anything about *talking* to her.

"What are you guys doing after school?" Andie asked, staring into the back of Cate's lavender polo.

"Your optimism is cute, C.C.," Cate cooed, not bothering to turn around. "But I'm never going to invite you to hang out with the Chi Beta Phis."

Andie kicked a crushed Pepsi can on the sidewalk.

"Don't worry," Stella replied, shooting Andie a smile. "You're not missing much."

"I was thinking, Stella," Cate said, pushing her oversize Guccis onto the top of her head. "You may want to consider joining the marching band. They accept *everyone*." She turned onto Ninetieth Street, nearly punting a teacup Yorkie across the sidewalk.

Girls in charcoal gray wool skirts were crowded around Ashton Prep's entrance. The eight-story renovated mansion was surrounded by a small landscaped courtyard. Addison Isaacs and Missy Hurst were standing just inside the wrought iron gates, hugging each other and shrieking excitedly. At the top of the steps, two men in navy blazers stood on either side of the massive carved wood doors like bouncers, ushering uniform-clad upper-school girls inside. Molly Lambert, one of Ashton's only goths, sat on a bench in the corner of the courtyard, drawing on her hand with a black Sharpie.

"Thanks for your concern," Stella said breezily, pushing past a group of ninth-graders. "But I'll be brilliant on my own."

With that, she disappeared into the crowded courtyard.

Cate shook her head dismissively at Stella's retreating back. She strolled confidently toward the upper-school entrance, where Priya, Sophie, and Blythe were waiting for her. The lower and upper schools were in two separate wings, with separate entrances and separate lunchrooms.

Andie gazed longingly at Cate's friends. They were all wearing Lacoste button-downs in pastel shades of pink, blue, lavender, and green, like a handful of Easter M&M's. Betsy Carmichael was staring bug-eyed into the *Ashton News* camera, held by a twiggy sixth-grader with stringy black hair. Betsy kept up a running commentary on Chi Beta Phi's outfits, as though the courtyard were a Hollywood red carpet.

"Andie!" Cindy Ng called. She smiled wide, revealing perfectly straight, braces-free teeth.

Andie pulled Cindy into a tight hug, breathing in her Chanel Chance perfume. "You look awesome."

As they started toward the lower-school entrance, Andie heard a car horn blare. She turned to see Lola kneeling on the street in front of a mustard yellow cab, a few books scattered on the ground by her feet. The driver was hanging out the window, shaking his fist at her. This morning Lola had had to borrow one of Andie's uniform skirts, which was so short she was flashing her days-of-the-week underwear.

"Who's that?" Cindy asked, cringing.

Andie was about to answer when Cate pushed by, Betsy Carmichael and the *Ashton News* camera in tow. Blythe, Sophie, and Priya were following close behind them, their hands covering their mouths in amusement.

"Ladies of Ashton Prep!" Cate called out, laughing. She stood by the sidewalk and framed Lola with her hands. "Meet Lola Childs!"

Blythe pulled Cate away and the girls took off up the stairs and into the Upper School, erupting in a fit of giggles.

Betsy Carmichael stood in front of Lola and stared into the camera. "Welcome back, Ashton Prep girls. I'm Betsy Carmichael, telling you to keep it hot, keep it fresh, and keep it real."

As Andie watched Lola fumble with her books, her face as red as a tomato, her stomach sank with guilt. The last thing Lola needed was another sister torturing her—that was the last thing *either* of them needed.

"I'll see you in English," Andie said to Cindy. "I'll explain later."

She pushed through the small crowd that had formed on the sidewalk. When she got to her, Lola was still struggling with her books.

"Hey . . ." Andie said slowly.

"I'm fine," Lola mumbled, but even as she said it she dropped her leather-bound *Ashton Prep's Code of Ethics* on the ground. She picked it up, but the back of her skirt was standing up straight, stiff with starch. Hannah Marcus, a seventh-grader who refused to play sports because she "didn't like to sweat," pointed at Lola and cackled.

"Here," Andie said, smoothing the skirt back down. "I'll walk you to homeroom." She took a few books from Lola's hands.

"Thanks," Lola said, standing up a little straighter.

Andie pushed past Hannah and shot her a dirty look. Maybe she and Lola weren't going to be best friends, but as of next Sunday they were family. And Andie wasn't going to let anyone—Cate or otherwise—treat her family like that.

BANISHED TO LOSERVILLE

Stella took a bite of her turkey burger and glanced around Ashton Prep's crowded cafeteria. Its long oak tables were filled with uniform-clad girls, gossiping over plates of grilled chicken and brown rice sushi. In the corner two bony freshman girls were eating nothing but vanilla frozen yogurt. Everyone was sitting with someone else—everyone except Stella.

Stella looked down the end of her table, where the Ashton field hockey team was discussing their "sweeper." All day, she'd overheard girls talking about Shelley DeWitt's house in the Hamptons, some people called Dean and DeLuca, or the brunch Eleanor Donner threw every year at her grandmother's Upper West Side town house. Ashton Prep girls spoke a different language, some sort of elite code their mothers must have taught them when they were babies. Stella wished the headmistress had given her a pocket translator, instead of that useless handbook with five whole pages dedicated to the proper way to outfit the school uniform—as if anyone actually paid attention to those rules.

No matter where Stella was—Kensington Gardens, the Nanette Lepore store, or the French Riviera—people always flocked to her. But so far at Ashton Prep she'd only talked to three teachers and the cafeteria lady who'd asked her, "Fries or salad?" But she wasn't about to give up that easily. Stella straightened up and leaned toward the field hockey girls. She glanced at the least sporty-looking girl at the table, who had glossy long brown hair.

Just then Cate waltzed in, her chin held high, flanked by the Chi Beta Phis. Every head in the lunchroom turned as they sat down at a table by the window.

"Do you think they're letting anyone else in this year?" a girl with dyed blue bangs asked the rest of the team.

"If they do, it would probably be Kirsten Phillips," a girl with splotchy red cheeks answered definitively. "Last year they invited her to have dinner with them at Ono."

Stella sat back in her seat, wishing she had Bose sound-canceling headphones. In gym, two girls had spent the entire volleyball game discussing a rumor that Cate had chartered a yacht to Miami this summer by herself, hosting a port-to-port party. She was starting to think Cate was right: If you weren't one of the Chi Beta Phis, you were a nobody.

A short blond girl with a faint white mustache walked toward the table and sat down across from Stella. She pulled all the contents from her pockets and set them down on her tray. "Ahh, that feels better," she said, to no one in particular. There was a tube of ChapStick, some tissues, and a key chain that said, DON'T DRINK AND DERIVE. Her monogrammed L.L. Bean backpack said *M.U.G.* Stella glanced over at Cate's table, where all the girls were now huddled close together, as though they were studying a treasure map of Barneys' secret floor.

"You're new here," the girl said, opening up a packet of Sweet'N Low and pouring it over her macaroni and cheese.

"Um, yeah," Stella said. Mustache Girl took a bite of macaroni covered in white powder.

"I'm Myra, Myra Granberry."

Stella sunk into her chair. She could suddenly imagine her life at Ashton Prep—she wouldn't be alone after all. She and Myra would be best mates. Stella would get a matching L.L. Bean backpack, eat Chef Boyardee with Equal, and spend Friday nights waxing Myra's mustache or feeding Myra's sea monkeys—or, if she was lucky—both.

Across the lunchroom, Cate watched Stella as Myra Granberry petted her furry upper lip.

"Come on, Cate," Priya said, following Cate's gaze. She broke up a neon green wasabi ball with her chopsticks. "You can't let her sit in Loserville with M.U.G. the Slug."

"Actually, I can," Cate snapped. She glanced at Blythe for support and caught her rolling her eyes. "That's funny," Cate growled, staring down at her sushi. "I didn't order an eye roll."

"Sorry." Blythe shrugged, looking to Priya and Sophie. "But what's the big deal about her sitting with us?"

Cate gripped the edge of the table. "We have rules!" she snapped. She stared across the crowded lunchroom. Beth Ann Pinchowski was picking a tray off a giant stack by the door, her

Converse All Stars barely covering her ugly ankle socks. "Doesn't anyone remember Beth Ann? We let her hang out with us in sixth grade and a week later she was dragging us to *Finding Nemo on Ice!*"

She'd tried to get them all to wear bright orange hats that looked like Nemo, with little fins sticking out the sides. But it was *Cate* who'd had to plan Operation Phase-Out, eventually forcing Beth Ann to leave the group.

"That was different," Sophie said, shaking her head. She was staring at Stella sympathetically, as though Myra were about to force-feed her boogers.

"It was pretty bad, though," Priya noted. The girls watched as Beth Ann took out a Kleenex and blew her nose. It sounded like a motorcycle revving its engine. "I really don't want to see any more shows on ice—do you?"

Sophie shook her head slowly.

Blythe shrugged. "Okay, so it's just us. Whatever."

Cate sat back in her chair, satisfied. Ashton Prep was *her* school, the Chi Beta Phis were *her* friends, and *she* made the rules. And from now on Cate was enforcing a strict closed-door policy: No Brits allowed.

THE FROG PRINCE

Lola strolled down Eighty-second Street Monday after school. She hadn't seen Andie since she dropped her off at homeroom, and she'd spent the day feeling helpless and alone, like the geeky girl in some after-school special. In world history, a cute blond girl had asked the teacher if the Ashton Prep uniform included days-of-the-week knickers. Everywhere she went, it seemed like people were whispering about her and giggling behind her back.

The afternoon sun warmed up her body and she smiled as she turned down Fifth Avenue, remembering where she was headed. She couldn't wait to see Kyle. He'd promised her a "first day of school" ice cream after his band practice, just like old times.

Lola approached the Mister Softee truck on the corner, where a little boy with a fruit punch mustache waited in line with his mother. Across the street, two muscular guys were break dancing on a sheet of cardboard outside Central Park. Lola waited patiently. Any minute, Kyle would be pulling his baritone horn up the street on his hand trolley, with his too-big-for-his-face glasses. She smiled just thinking about him.

"Sticks!" an unfamiliar voice called out her old nickname. Lola turned back to the ice cream truck. In front of it stood . . .

"*Kyle*?" she squeaked.

The boy standing before her was almost unrecognizable. Kyle had filled out and gotten a tan, and he wasn't wearing his glasses. His brown eyes twinkled against his dewy skin. His hair was still spiky, but less Harry Potter dorky and more Zac Efron hottie. And . . . he was *tall*.

"Hey!" Kyle grinned as he handed the man in the truck a few wrinkled bills. The man set them in a battered shoe box, gently patting his sweaty forehead with a single.

Lola stepped toward Kyle, her long skinny legs feeling suddenly unsteady. She eyed the black guitar case slung over his back. "Um, what happened to your baritone horn?" she asked stupidly.

Kyle laughed and pushed his bangs off his forehead. "Oh man, I forgot about that thing. I've been playing guitar for the last couple years."

Lola untucked her blond hair from her ears. Across the street, one of the break-dancers spun around on his head.

"You still play the viola?" Kyle asked, taking two chocolate cones from the man's hands. Chocolate ice cream and Fanta orange soda had always been their favorites. Bonus points if had together.

"I do!" Lola said, her voice a little shrill. She stared into Kyle's warm brown eyes, suddenly nervous. She could feel the sweat pooling at the small of her back. She glanced at Kyle's ankles for reassurance, but the white tube socks and Tevas he used to wear had been replaced with Adidas sneakers.

Kyle handed her a cone and Lola grabbed for it quickly, knocking it into the front of his shirt. The cone smashed onto the ground, leaving a trail of brown sludge behind it.

Lola pulled a tissue from her pink Gap purse and pressed it to his shirt. It fell apart, leaving huge white papery clumps. "Oh, no . . ."

She brought her hands to her freckled face and stared at the sidewalk. The chocolate puddle inched toward her Reef flip-flops.

"I guess some things never change, Sticks." Kyle laughed, pulling the wet fabric away from his chest.

A group of Ashton Prep girls crossed the street toward the park. A redhead with a squished face pointed over her shoulder at Kyle and the other girls stole glances at him.

Lola's whole body felt like it had been set on fire, her skin hot and red. It was obvious what they were saying: *Who on earth is Kyle Lewis with? And more importantly, um, why?*

And suddenly, Lola asked herself the same thing.

They'd met up less than five minutes ago, but already Kyle could be filed under PEOPLE WHO WILL NOT BE SEEN IN PUBLIC WITH LOLA CHILDS, right next to Stella, Cate, and everyone else in New York City.

A VILLIAN IN THEORY

Stella sat in the den, doodling aimlessly in her sketchbook. Not only had she sat with Myra at lunch, but in bio they'd been paired up as lab partners, where she'd overheard whispering and learned Myra's unfortunate nickname. Stella imagined standing onstage at the science fair, in front of a poster titled HEMORRHAGIC FEVER. Myra would grip her hand, the entire school chanting, *M.U.G. the Slug! M.U.G. the Slug!*

The entire day Cate had watched Stella roam the halls like a mental patient, stumbling confused into the wrong classrooms. She'd even pretended she didn't know her in study hall, when the teacher sat them next to one another.

Stella sat back on the leather couch and sighed. She was Stella *Childs*, spawn of a supermodel and a duke. She'd grown up going to fashion shows and movie premieres, and her sketches had once been displayed at a gallery in Notting Hill. She was supposed to be on top of the high school food chain—not discussing bioterrorism with a bottom-feeder. But short of announcing to all of Ashton Prep, *I'm practically royalty, please worship me!*, she was out of ideas.

Whether she liked it or not, she needed Cate—and admittance to the Chi Beta Phis.

Just then, Cate breezed past the French doors, her black-and-white Balenciaga bag swinging on her shoulder. "So long, *sis*," she said smugly. "I'm meeting Blythe at Barneys."

Stella crumpled the sketch she was working on, annoyed. But then she had an idea.

"I know it's none of my business," Stella heard herself say. "But you should really watch your back."

Cate leaned on the door frame and narrowed her eyes. "What's that supposed to mean?"

"Blythe's not happy being second-in-command anymore, especially with her two new assets." Stella stared at her seriously. So it was an exaggeration. But Blythe *had* seemed a little annoyed with Cate at the sleepover. And it was a well-known fact that once girls sprouted boobs, they totally changed. Besides, Stella couldn't hang out with M.U.G. the Slug for the next four years. This was an emergency.

"What makes you such an expert on Blythe's happiness?" Cate asked suspiciously.

"I didn't say I was an expert. It's just that we have French together and . . ." Stella trailed off, pretending to be so engrossed in her sketch she couldn't possibly finish her sentence.

"And what?" Cate demanded.

"Nothing. Forget I said anything."

"You think Blythe wants to lead the Chi Beta Phis?"

Stella shrugged noncommittally, knowing she'd done enough.

"There's safety in numbers," she continued. "You could always let me in. You know, for security. Just something to think about."

"I thought you were '*brilliant*' on your own?" Cate asked, faking a British accent.

Stella studied her cuticles. "Suit yourself. I was just trying to help."

Cate turned to leave but stopped at the top of the stairs. She ran her tongue over her teeth thoughtfully. Blythe *had* spent all of bio talking about what a pain it was to buy all new clothes, since nothing fit her in the chest anymore. And then there was that eye roll at lunch. . . .

"I'll think about it," she called over her shoulder.

Cate followed Blythe through Chelsea Passage, the home department at Barneys. Blythe touched a tall cream-colored vase. It was completely smooth except for a large elephant trunk coming out of its center.

"What about this?" she giggled.

"Nice," Cate teased, glancing around for an engagement/wedding/thank-you-for-ruining-my-life gift for Emma and her dad. One wall was covered in plates with graphic faces, like an artful police lineup. A stack of red and yellow mod plastic chairs sat in one corner, next to a long pink table set with neon yellow china.

"Or how about this?" Blythe pointed to a red glass vase with a nose and a handlebar moustache.

"Eh . . . not so much," Cate murmured.

"Come on! It's funny!" Blythe said, pulling her freshly high-lighted hair into a ponytail.

A saleswoman with a wannabe-Rihanna bob shot the girls a dirty look. Cate shot her a look right back. This was Barneys—not the library.

The truth was, she didn't care about buying her dad and Emma a gift anymore. She'd spent the last hour dissecting everything Blythe had done since she'd been back from Greece. Why had she let Sophie borrow her hoop earrings? Why had she asked Priya to go to the bathroom with her during gym? Was that paper she'd passed to Mackenzie Brooks during history more than just the homework? Was she announcing the new regime?

"What did you do last night?" Cate asked casually, wandering over to a wall of picture frames. She rubbed her hand over a black alligator frame. It felt rough to the touch.

"Nothing." Blythe picked up a lacquered Mondrian box and turned it over in her hands.

"You didn't do a single thing?" Cate pressed, hoping the question sounded innocent.

"Fine, I went to dinner with my mom."

Cate watched her, unsure whether she had just caught Blythe in a lie. She shook her head and sighed. "Let's go upstairs," she announced, heading for the escalators. "Forget the wedding. I'm in the market for a new dress."

Blythe picked a piece of lint off Cate's gray uniform skirt as they stepped on the escalator. "I wish you could have come to

Greece this summer. I had to hang out with Connor the whole time. I'm now fluent in two-year-old."

Cate laughed despite herself, picturing super-tan Blythe and Connor on the beaches of Santorini, Blythe buried up to her neck in sand. Blythe's father had remarried after her parents divorced, and now he lived with his new wife and son in L.A., where he produced big-budget action films and little blond babies.

Cate stepped off the escalator, a little relieved. Maybe Stella was wrong. Blythe seemed to be the same as always, making Cate laugh between spray tans.

On the sixth floor, an army of Marc by Marc Jacobs mannequins was posed in a line, racks of brightly colored clothing adorning the walls behind them. She loved how Barneys had no aisles, just open space and walls lined with exquisite clothes—exactly how a store should be. Beth Ann Pinchowski had dragged the girls to Macy's once, and Cate had nearly had a panic attack from the masses of tourists and the claustrophobia-inducing, tightly packed clothing racks. Blythe had handed her a paper shopping bag and instructed her to slowly breathe in and out.

Cate walked along a lime green wall covered with bags and shoes, running her fingers over a chocolate brown Sissi Rossi tote. Across the store, Ally Pierce, an Ashton senior, was holding a gold lamé tunic. Interesting—were metallics back? Cate made a mental note to share the tidbit with the girls.

"So, Priya said her sister said that if we have to choose between sculpture and band next term, we should choose sculpture." Cate picked up the buttery leather tote and slung it over her shoulder experimentally.

"Yeah, she mentioned that to me too." Blythe circled a tropical fish tank with a giant smiling Buddha inside. A snail crawled across his chubby belly. "She said they get models from the Lincoln Center ballet company. Even in tights, the guys are super cute."

Cate dropped the bag on the ground. Priya definitely hadn't mentioned anything about *male models*. Cate had always been the one to get feedback on their collective schedules, then make final decisions about registering. She needed that kind of information. And when had Priya even *talked* to Blythe about sculpture? Cate had been in every class with them. Every class except French. . . .

"I just thought we should finalize our plans," Cate said, trying to compose herself. She followed Blythe over to the Theory rack along the wall.

"Sounds good." Blythe pulled a bright blue cashmere V-neck off the rack and held it up to her boobs. They looked even bigger than they had yesterday. "I'm going to try this on—meet me in the dressing room upstairs." She turned and walked toward the glass stairs.

Meet me in the dressing room upstairs? That sounded like an order. Cate didn't respond to those.

Cate lingered by the Theory rack far longer than she needed to, watching as a woman with stiff red hair set a Louis Vuitton suitcase on the counter and returned its contents—twelve different beige purses. Finally, Cate pulled a few dresses from the rack and headed upstairs too.

Blythe was admiring every angle of herself in the dressing

room's three-way mirror. "Verdict?" she asked, turning to the side. She twisted her highlighted hair into a ponytail and the sweater rode up, revealing a slice of toned orange stomach.

"Guilty of making your boobs look huge," Cate blurted out. It looked like Blythe had shoved two water balloons in her shirt, the way they used to in third grade, playing in Carl Schurz Park on the East River.

"I know!" Blythe cried excitedly, pushing back her bangs. "I look hot!" She winked at her reflection. Cate looked down at her tiny chest, which just barely filled out her padded A cups.

"Can I start a room for you?" a voice asked.

Cate turned to see a college-age girl in bright green stilettos, ten silver hoops hugging one ear.

"Actually . . ." Cate said, forcing a smile. The clothes slung over her arm suddenly felt like they weighed five hundred pounds. "I'm not in the mood to try anything on. I'll just take these."

The girl nodded and turned to go. "By the way, that's perfect on you," she added, admiring Blythe's sweater.

"Thanks," Blythe said smugly. Then she looked over her shoulder at Cate and smiled.

Fifteen minutes and five Theory purchases later, Cate and Blythe pushed through Barneys revolving glass doors and stepped out onto Madison Avenue. Cate started to take off toward Sixty-first Street, two shopping bags swinging at her side. But Blythe didn't move.

"I have to run errands downtown," she said. Her face was pink and expressionless.

"What errands?" Cate pressed, resting a hand on the waist of her uniform skirt.

"Just some stuff—I better hurry." Blythe glanced at her bare orange wrist.

"Blythe!" Cate yelled, as Blythe took off down the street, her Tory Burch flats thwacking against the sidewalk. "You don't even wear a watch!"

"See you tomorrow!" Blythe called, not looking back. Cate's legs felt like they were Krazy Glued to the sidewalk. Blythe was keeping secrets from her—she just *knew* it. Blythe, her so-called best friend, her second-in-command. How *could* she?

She whipped out her iPhone and dialed Sophie's number. Her call went straight to voice mail.

"Sophie, call me as soon as you get this, we need to talk," Cate snapped, clutching the phone to her ear. Sophie always kept her phone on, even when she was playing with her Barbies.

A red double-decker bus barreled past. On the roof, a girl wearing a foam Statue of Liberty crown stared down at Cate as though she were an exotic animal.

She dialed Priya next. *This is Priya,* her voice mail cooed. *Do your thing.*

Cate didn't bother leaving a message. It was obvious what was going on. Blythe had made plans with Sophie and Priya and not invited her. Why else would they both have their phones off?

So Stella had been right after all. Blythe wasn't loyal. She'd just been studying Cate these past three years, making a huge folder labeled HOW TO OVERTHROW THE CHI BETA PHI PRESIDENT.

IF AT FIRST YOU DON'T SUCCEED, TRY, TRY AGAIN

Andie paced back and forth across her room, hugging a bright orange throw pillow to her chest like a life preserver. She hadn't been so nervous since Ben Carter asked her to be his girlfriend last fall.

She looked at the piece of paper on her desk one final time. She had bulleted out all her points and memorized them, like she had for her history report last year. Technically she was supposed to be helping Emma pick out centerpieces, but there was no reason she couldn't bring up her modeling career while comparing peonies and roses.

She would start by telling Emma how modeling was her destiny.

If Emma said she was too young, she'd remind her that she herself had been thirteen when she shot her first Calvin Klein ad.

If she said Andie was too petite, she'd argue that Kate Moss was five-foot six—short for a model!

If she said the business was tough, she'd tell her her skin was thicker than a vintage Yves Saint Laurent alligator purse.

She'd leave out the fact that she'd submitted photos of herself with her contact information to the Ford website and that they hadn't called back. They probably never checked the site anyway.

Then she would ask Emma if she could go to Fashion Week at Bryant Park with her. Emma had been so busy running around with Gloria, deciding on tablecloths and what paper stock she wanted for thank-you notes, she was missing most of the week's events. But she had to go to the Ralph Lauren show tomorrow afternoon. And with a little luck, Andie would be her plus-one.

The beige plastic intercom on the wall crackled. "Andie, Gloria is here with the flowers," Emma's voice cooed.

Andie raced down the stairs and into the kitchen. Emma was standing next to the granite island and talking on her cell phone. "I realize that," Emma said into her phone, "but it's an inconvenience."

Andie stood in the doorway, frozen. No matter how many times she passed Emma in the hall or ate oatmeal across from her, she was always a little starstruck. It was like finding the Jonas Brothers in your bathroom.

The granite kitchen island was covered with flowers. An older woman stood next to Emma, running her mauve fingernails through her thinning brown hair. Her skin was bizarrely taut.

"Gloria Rubenstein," the woman announced, taking Andie's hand in her own. "They say I'm one of the best party planners in New York—and *they* are right." Gloria let out a little laugh, her eyes wide open as though she were surprised.

Andie glanced at Emma, who was still on the phone. "Right,"

Emma said, sounding annoyed. She pressed her finger against her temple. She set the cell phone on the counter and looked at Andie and Gloria apologetically. "I'm so sorry, I'm afraid we have to postpone this—apparently Winston and I have to be at a tasting at the boathouse in half an hour."

Andie pulled at the hem of her skirt, disappointed. The Ralph Lauren show was less than a day away, and she'd been waiting all summer to talk to Emma about modeling. But every time she'd chickened out. Today was going to be the day. She stared into Emma's face, the same one she'd seen on the side of every New York City bus during the Chanel No. 5 campaign. "No problem," she said brightly, forcing a smile.

"Thank you for understanding." Emma grabbed her cropped trench from off a kitchen stool. Gloria waved a hand, as if used to dealing with flighty, overbooked clients.

"I'll make it up to you," Emma promised Andie as she headed out the front door.

Andie trudged up the stairs, just as Gloria's cell rang.

"Romando! Darling!" Gloria cried loudly. "Tell me you're available to shoot Sunday. It's *Emma Childs's* wedding—*you* should be paying *us.*"

Andie walked upstairs and paced outside of Winston's old office. The decorators had painted the walls a mustard color and put a queen-size bed by the window. The door of Stella's closet was open, a pile of brown boxes stacked next to it like a giant Jenga tower.

"Stella?" Andie finally asked, her voice a little squeaky. She hadn't been able to stop thinking about the *Allure* article with

Stella—the girl who said Paulina was practically her aunt. If Emma couldn't get her into Fashion Week, maybe *Stella* could. She crept over to the closet, where Stella was kneeling on the floor, opening a cardboard box that said STELLA HAIR PRODUCTS.

Stella sat back on her heels, holding two bottles of Frédéric Fekkai shampoo in her hands like barbells. "Bollocks," she mumbled, glancing up at Andie. "I've gone through my entire room twice and I'm still missing two boxes—Beauty Supplies and Dress Tops Three," she explained. "And I can't find any of my charcoals."

"Stella . . ." Andie said slowly, leaning against the door frame, "Last year I read that article in—"

"Did the movers put any boxes in your room?" Stella interrupted, pushing past Andie and digging through another box on the top of the stack.

"No . . ." Andie said, pressing on. "I guess I just wanted to—"

Stella threw down a pair of Anlo jeans and put her hands on her hips. "Now is not a good time, C.C.," she sighed. "I'm in crisis mode." She disappeared back into the closet and lifted up a pair of Jimmy Choo heels, as if a cardboard box could be hiding underneath them.

Andie stepped back, stung. *C.C.* She had been hoping that was filed in the back of Stella's brain, along with every other thing Cate had called her (*midget, wannabe, poser, Munchkin*). But apparently it was right up there, front and center.

She walked out of Stella's room, defeated. She'd been silly for thinking she could talk to Stella about modeling—three days might have passed, but nothing had changed.

. . .

Stella sprawled out on her bed, staring at the ornate crown molding. Clothes and boxes were spread out on her floor, like her closet had thrown up all over her room. Not only did she have zero friends in New York, now she didn't have any dress tops, either. Not that she felt like wearing them, anyway. She'd texted Bridget and Pippa five times, but it was nearly twelve o'clock in London, and neither of them had answered. She tugged at a golden blond ringlet until her scalp hurt.

Someone cleared her throat. Lola was perched in the doorway, scanning the room as though Stella were the victim of some horrible natural disaster. In her hand was a small bag from somewhere called Duane Reade.

"Does this look like your room?" Stella muttered, sitting up.

"Sorry," Lola said quietly. She stared at the ripped cardboard box in the corner. "What are you doing?"

"Mourning the loss of my favorite Madison Marcus silk top." Stella frowned. Then she narrowed her eyes at Lola. "Did you steal a box of mine?"

"No, no." Lola shook her head. "I already unpacked my clothes." She wandered into Stella's room, stepping over a colorful pile of Chanel nail polishes. On Stella's dresser was a framed photo of their family from Boxing Day. They all had thin paper crowns on their head in light green, purple, and pink. Lola pressed her finger into her dad's grinning face, feeling like she'd swallowed a brick. It had taken a month before they'd found out about Cloud.

Lola smoothed down her frizzy hair and turned to Stella, chewing the ChapStick off her bottom lip. "Stella?" she asked. She wanted to tell her about the cab incident this morning, and how'd she'd eaten her lunch in the courtyard with Birdy, one of the Ashton security guards. She wanted to tell her how Kyle—geeky, I-shoot-peas-out-of-my-nose-at-dinner Kyle—was cool now. And more than anything, she wanted to ask how Stella could walk by that picture every day and not feel like she'd been run over by a tank. She set the frame facedown on the dresser.

Stella leaned back against her headboard, watching Lola's freckled nose. It always twitched when she was about to cry. She knew that Lola hated talking about their dad—she hadn't said a word about him all summer in Tuscany, and refused to talk to him whenever he called. It made it easier for Stella to be nice to him—Lola was mad enough for the both of them. Yes, he had made a massive mistake, but he was still their dad.

Just then Stella's iPhone blared its techno ring. She picked up the phone and looked at the vibrating screen. Cate.

"Lola," she said holding up one finger. "I have to get this, hold on." She picked up her mobile. "Hello?" she asked. Cate had only ever called her once—and that had been three days ago.

"What are you doing?" Cate asked.

"Just unpacking my clothes—"

"Alone?"

Stella eyed Lola, who had walked back toward the door, swinging the red and blue Duane Reade bag around her thin wrist. "Of course I'm alone," Stella muttered. "Do you have to rub it in?"

Lola stopped swinging the bag and looked at Stella, her nose twitching again. Stella tried to mouth the word *sorry*, but Lola stormed out of the room.

"Thanks for the intel before," Cate continued. "I've decided you can hang out with us. But it has to be on *my* terms."

"Fine," Stella replied, not really sure what "my terms" meant. But before she could ask, Cate had hung up.

TO: Blythe Finley, Priya Singh, Sophie Sachs
FROM: Cate Sloane
DATE: Monday, 9:18 p.m.
SUBJECT: Democracy Now

Listen up, ladies!

As official leader of the Chi Beta Phis, it's my duty to ensure that all prospective members go through a screening process more rigorous than the CIA's. I refuse to have you subjected to any more shows on ice.

At our last sleepover, you asked if we could hang out with my stepsister, Stella Childs. Now, I'm answering: yes. For the next five days Stella will be "in trials." I'll give her a series of tasks to see if she is Chi Beta Phi material, and on Saturday (assuming she completes all her trials) we'll vote to see if she should be in.

Be discerning!
Cate

A SISTER IN NEED IS A FRIEND INDEED

Lola studied her reflection in the bathroom mirror and frowned. She pulled on the teal cloth headband she'd bought at Duane Reade after her disastrous reunion with Kyle. Two years had transformed him into the most adorable guy she'd ever seen, but she was still his mate Sticks. She still had big ears and a bump in the middle of her nose. And she still couldn't last ten minutes without spilling soda on her jumper or stepping in a steaming pile of dog poo.

She adjusted the headband so it concealed the tips of her ears. From now on, things would be different. *She* would be different. No more tripping over things. And absolutely no more Dumbo ears.

Andie peeked into the bathroom. She was wearing plaid pajama pants that looked three sizes too big. "I just need to wash my face," she said, sidling up next to the sink.

"About today," Lola started. Before leaving her at homeroom, Andie had drawn a map on the back of her schedule so Lola would know where all her classes were. "Thanks for helping me." Her stomach hurt just thinking about her debut on *Ashton News*.

"No problem." Andie eyed Lola's hair and the Duane Reade bag crumpled up by the sink. "What's with the headband?"

"I just thought . . ." Lola watched as Andie leaned over and lathered up her face. She hesitated, not wanting to reveal too much. But even if Andie did have an intimidatingly perfect wardrobe, gorgeous never-frizzy hair, and a button nose, she wasn't going to make fun of Lola in front of the entire school. "I thought that maybe it would hide my ears."

"What's wrong with your ears?" Andie asked, splashing her face with water. She already knew the answer to that question, but after today she figured Lola could use a little self-esteem boost.

Lola chewed her lower lip. "Well, they're big. And . . . well, there's this bloke Kyle, who I grew up with in London. We've been talking online all summer and he lives in Tribeca now."

Andie patted her face with a checkered towel, her lips curling into a smile. "Let me guess: You like him?"

Lola blushed so much her big ears turned red. Kyle was one of the cutest guys she'd ever seen, *and* he was nice. And funny and smart and all-around wonderful. "It doesn't matter," Lola mumbled. "He'd never fancy me."

"But you've been talking to him online all summer, right?" Andie asked, walking back into her room. Lola nodded. Andie plopped down on her bed and pulled a bright red throw pillow into her arms. "That's a good start. Now you just need to get out of the friend zone," she said matter-of-factly.

"But how?" Lola asked, walking to the door.

"You just stop being his friend and lay on the *girl*." Andie twirled her ponytail around her finger as she said "girl." Lola was still standing tentatively in the doorway. "You can come in, you know."

Lola glanced around the room, which had one bright red wall. Almost every surface—the chaise lounge, the bed, the desk chair—was decorated with brightly colored Moroccan pillows. It felt like an exotic palace, minus the belly dancers.

Above Andie's head was a massive collage. In the center hung a black-and-white photo of a woman holding a baby. Ticket stubs to *Wicked* and *Rent* were sandwiched between a cartoon of a Siamese cat doing yoga and a glossy pullout of David and Victoria Beckham, modeling their signature dVb line. Beside it was a Chloé ad featuring a model covered in leather handbags, as though an avalanche of accessories had tumbled down on her. Andie's smiling face was pasted on the body. It looked like she had no neck. Lola giggled.

Andie followed Lola's gaze and quickly stood up on the bed. "You weren't supposed to see that." She pulled the ad from the collage and tucked it into the drawer in her nightstand.

"I'm sorry, it's just—why did you do that?" Lola squeezed the ends of her frizzy hair and tried to stop smiling.

"It's really not funny." Andie knew Lola didn't mean anything by it, but she was careful who she told about modeling. She didn't want Cate to know she was actually serious about it—not until there was something to prove it was real.

"I'm so sorry," Lola repeated, pressing her hands into her freckled cheeks. She looked from the collage to Andie's nightstand, which had more fashion magazines than a nail salon—and what looked like a printout of the FordModels.com home page. Understanding washed over her face. "Do you want to model?"

Andie bit her cuticle. "I know, it's totally dumb. I'm four-foot eleven. But Nurse Paul said I'm due for a growth spurt this year—and I've been drinking a lot of milk."

"No, no," Lola protested, gazing at Andie's round, flawless face. "I don't think it's dumb at all. You're prettier than most of those girls in *Teen Vogue*." Lola meant it.

"Thanks," Andie said, lying back on her bed. "I tried to talk to your mom about it, but she had to go to a tasting at the boathouse and she's not back yet. I really wanted her to take me to Fashion Week—I would honestly lick Cate's feet if I could be in the same room as Kate Moss," she said wistfully.

"Ew! You don't need to do that." She clapped her hands together in front of her face, small and fast. "Let's just sneak in! I've been to the shows before—it can't be that hard."

Andie's eyes widened. *Lola.* She'd thought Emma would help her, and that Stella was the next best thing. But Lola was a Childs too. Andie had totally overlooked her—in more ways than one.

Andie grinned, picturing herself sitting front row, watching as Bar Refaeli strutted down the runway in a Cynthia Rowley couture gown. "Yes!" she cried, pulling Lola into a tight hug.

She'd rub shoulders with Anna Wintour and smile at Heidi Klum. She'd absorb fashion and exude modeling vibes. And maybe, just *maybe*, she'd get . . . discovered.

TRIALS AND TRIBULATIONS

Stella followed Cate down an air-conditioned corridor that smelled vaguely of Elmer's glue. On the way to school this morning, Cate had kept on about Blythe's new knockers, even referring to her as B.B. (Boobie Blythe). Then she'd pulled Stella out of homeroom to give her an "official" Ashton Prep tour. Stella couldn't wait to walk down the hall first period with the Chi Beta Phis.

Forget M.U.G. the Slug—she'd moved on to bigger and better acronyms.

They mounted a narrow cherry staircase and turned down a wide hallway. Abstract wire sculptures that looked like giant copper amoebas lined the walls. A tall girl with a bouffant, *Hairspray* chorus-girl hairdo and white eyeliner came out of one of the rooms. Her gray apron was stained with dark red splotches, like she'd just completed a Jackson Pollock–style painting using only ketchup.

"Hi, Cate," she called.

"Hey, Missy. This is Stella," Cate responded.

Stella straightened up. Maybe Blythe wasn't really drawing up plans for a coup, but that one teensy lie had been worth it. For the first time since school started, she wasn't the odd girl out.

"Hey." Missy smiled as she walked past.

"Missy's in eleventh grade," Cate whispered as they turned down a corridor. In a room with red leather sofas, a few girls were sprawled out on the floor, scribbling on an oversize GET WELL card with a bedridden zebra on the front. "She's an amazing artist—she was the youngest person ever to get a piece in the Whitney. But the girl's got more issues than *Seventeen* magazine."

Cate paused. "I almost forgot," she said, crossing the room to a sliding glass door. "This is our deck."

Stella stepped outside onto a stone patio enclosed by a high wrought iron fence. "It's amazing," she breathed, spinning around. In front of her spread a giant patch of green—Central Park—lined by stately towers with granite facades. In the distance was the murky Hudson River, and beyond that, New Jersey—New York's loser cousin.

Cate crossed her arms over her chest. "So this week you'll have to complete a few . . . *trials*. And then on Saturday the Chi Beta Phis will vote on whether or not you should be admitted to the group."

Stella glanced around the deck, imagining eating seared tuna salads with the Chi Beta Phis and deciding what outfits to wear to the Ashton formal. She could handle a few trials, if that was what it took. Finally she nodded.

"Here's my offer," Cate continued. "You let me know if Blythe is acting suspicious, and I'll go easy on you for trials. Deal?"

"Abso-bloody-lutely." Stella followed Cate into the elevator, the gold railing shining under the overhead light. The doors opened and she stepped out into the oak-paneled hallway, walking a little faster, a bounce in her step. Ashton Prep was *her* school now. She would sit next to Priya in Latin, texting back and forth about the teacher's comb-over. She'd do yogalates with Sophie and Cate in gym, toning her core for a summer on Blythe's father's yacht. She'd hold a meet-and-greet in the drawing room, the Chi Beta Phis by her side as the entire ninth grade nervously introduced themselves to Stella Childs, Ashton's newest It girl.

As they reached geometry class, Stella spotted Priya and Blythe down the hall, leaning against the burgundy wall by the door. They both waved when they saw her coming. Stella tousled her golden ringlets, excited. "For your first trial," Cate said, shoving three heavy textbooks into her arms, "*you* carry my books." The books knocked Stella hard in the ribs.

Cate winked. "We have to make this believable. And I took the liberty of making a little 'to do' list for you." She took off toward Blythe and Priya and kissed them both on their cheeks.

Stella looked down at the stack of books, a piece of carnation pink paper tucked into the one on top. She closed her eyes, let out a deep breath, and slowly unwrapped the note.

FROM THE DESK OF CATE SLOANE

- Pick up the red Jimmy Choo flats on hold at Bergdorf's
  - —Lily, the saleswoman on the 5th floor should have them
  - —If Lily's not in today, Brianna—or Beatrice? (I can't remember) will definitely have them.
- Research venues for my birthday party in November
  - —Ono, Megu, and Tao are on the top of my list, but I need a few more options. Think fabulousness!
  - —I need digital photos of all venues uploaded to my Flickr account by tomorrow at 8 a.m.
  - —I also need to know what the menu would be like for a party of 50, 75, and 100.
- Call Frédéric Fekkai and book all my manicure, pedicure, and haircut appointments for the next year
  - —Manicures should be spaced a week apart, pedicures can be a week and a half apart, and haircuts should ALWAYS be four weeks apart (I have very temperamental follicles).

Stella frowned. Today she was carrying Cate's books and tomorrow she'd probably be pumicing Cate's feet with Bliss mint scrub during lunch. Whether or not her trials were "easy," one thing was certain—Cate Sloane was loving every minute of this.

BECOMING THE SWAN

Tuesday afternoon, Andie paced back and forth across Lola's room, her thin arms crossed over her chest. Lola needed some serious boy help, and Andie wasn't really sure where to start.

"First things first," Andie said, pausing in front of the bed, where Lola was sitting with Heath Bar in her lap. "You have to get rid of the furball."

"What? No!" Lola cried, clutching the cat tighter. He let out a sudden meow, like a sumo wrestler had just stepped on his tiny paw.

"Lola," Andie explained, "no boy is going to want to talk to you if you're holding a twenty-pound cat. You don't have to really get rid of him—just don't carry him around."

"Right, right," Lola said, kissing the cat on the head. She set him down gently on the floor and Heath Bar waddled into the bathroom, his big belly swinging.

Next Andie took in Lola's outfit, her gaze settling on her pale yellow Gap button-down. She riffled through her Alice + Olivia tote and pulled out a lint roller. She held it up high.

"That also means no cat hair—none. I bought this for you, so from now on you have to carry this wherever you go." Andie rolled the sleeve of Lola's shirt, then the back. "And no more touching that cat." She held the lint roller in front of Lola's face. It was covered in orange fur.

"But Heathy sleeps in my bed," Lola said sadly, running her hand over her bedspread.

Andie looked around Lola's room, pretending she hadn't heard that. After school she'd helped Lola unpack her books and hang up pictures of Starlett, her favorite horse from her stable in London. Her viola stood neatly in the corner, her CDs (mostly classical—Andie would have to work on that) were organized, and there was a photograph of Lola and her best friend, Abby, perched on the nightstand.

"So the next time you see Kyle, you want everything to go smoothly," Andie continued, putting her hands on her hips authoritatively. "You need a plan, from the second you see him. What are you going to do?"

Lola stared out the window, watching a one-legged pigeon hop along the stone ledge. "I guess I'd start with hello," Lola said thoughtfully. That felt like a safe answer.

"No!" Andie corrected her. "You're going to say . . ." Andie paused dramatically and tossed her glossy brown hair over her shoulder. "'Hi . . .'" She said it so softly it was practically a whisper.

Lola shook her head, her cheeks pink.

"Trust me," Andie continued. "I know what I'm talking about. I went out with Ben Carter last year for almost a month. *And* Clay Calhoun likes me—he's one of the hottest guys at Haverford." She wasn't bragging—it was true. Boys always liked her, and she never even had to try. Brett Crowley, a boy in her drawing class at the MoMA, had asked her out last year by sketching a picture of the Mona Lisa with her face on it. It wasn't exactly a faithful representation, but it was still cute.

"Oh," Lola said. She sat up a little straighter, impressed by Andie's credentials.

"Just practice it!" Andie coaxed.

"Hi . . ." Lola said softly, but when she tossed her hair, her headband slid down on her forehead.

"Okay . . . maybe we should start with more basic stuff," Andie amended. "You can't sweat or turn beet red when you talk to Kyle. And you can't be so clumsy—just move very slowly. If you're fumbling all the time, he'll know you like him."

Lola patted down her frizzy blond hair, confused. "But I *do* fancy him. . . ." Wasn't that the point? She wanted him to take her on a double-decker bus tour, or show her the inside of Belvedere castle, that spooky stone structure in Central Park.

"I know." Andie sighed. It was like Lola had been sick for all of fifth grade, when everyone else discovered boys *like* to be ignored. She put on her most patient face and took a deep breath. "But you don't want him to know that—at least not yet. You have to *pretend* like you don't care. If you get nervous, just pretend Kyle is . . ." Andie scanned the room. ". . . is Heath Bar!" The orange tabby was in the corner, licking the remnants of a glazed doughnut off a plate on Lola's nightstand.

Lola imagined herself on the double-decker tour bus, gazing into Heath Bar's furry face as they sped through Greenwich Village, the Washington Square arch flying past. She let out a laugh. It *would* be hard to get nervous if she did that.

Andie started pacing again, like a detective on the verge of solving a particularly tricky case. *The Case of Lola Childs and the Missing Cool Gene.* She stopped right in front of Lola. "And when you're walking next to each other, you always want to be within two feet of him. That way he'll be able to smell your perfume."

"But I don't wear perfume," Lola pointed out.

Andie pulled a tiny Philosophy bottle out of her bag and tossed it to Lola. "Now you do."

Lola sprayed the vanilla scent in the air and leaned forward into the mist. It smelled like cake batter, and she closed her eyes as she inhaled the sweet scent. But then she frowned.

"What's the problem?" Andie asked, one hand on her hip.

"Well, all this will only work if I actually see him again."

"And?"

"And after I spilled ice cream all over him, he said he had to go home and change his shirt." Lola filled her cheeks with air, like a blowfish on its guard. "I haven't heard from him since. And I'm not going to," she finished dejectedly, releasing the air from her cheeks.

Andie waved her hand dismissively. "Don't worry about it—that was only yesterday. Haven't you ever heard of boy time?"

Boy time was a well-proven unit of measurement. After Ben Carter had asked her for her phone number last year—via a note on a Bubblicious wrapper—he hadn't called for almost three days. Andie had been sick with worry until Cindy, whose favorite movie was *Clueless* despite the ugly '90s clothes, had reminded her about the golden rule revealed in the movie: Boys experience time differently. Sure enough, Ben had called on day three.

"And now for the most important part," she continued, taking Lola's MacBook from her desk and resting it on the bed. "Research." She looked disapprovingly at Lola's computer desktop: a photo of Heath Bar in a miniature construction paper party hat.

An IM popped up in the corner of the screen and Andie furrowed her brows. "Is Striker15 . . . *Kyle*?" She shot Lola an I-told-you-so look.

"Um . . . yes," Lola muttered. She leaned over the laptop and swallowed hard. Sure, she had been talking to Kyle online all summer, but now he was a real person. A real, *cute* person. They lived in the same city and she had just spilled ice cream all over his shirt. And apparently he still wanted to talk to her.

STRIKER15: HEY

She stared at the blinking cursor for a good long minute. Her fingers felt like they were made of lead. She reached to close the laptop.

"Just say hi!" Andie coaxed, sliding the MacBook in front of

Lola and opening it back up. Lola's palms started to sweat as she typed two letters onto the keyboard.

LOLABEAN: HI
STRIKER15: WHAT'S UP?

Lola bit her lip. She couldn't tell Kyle the truth—*Oh, I'm just sitting around learning how to make you like me.*

STRIKER15: WHAT'S THE MATTER? HEATH BAR GOT YR TONGUE? ☺

Lola looked stricken.

"Just ignore him for a minute. He's not going anywhere."

Andie rolled up the sleeves of her pale blue J. Crew button-down, her face serious. "Like I said, let's just do a little research." She pulled up Facebook and searched for "Kyle Lewis." A picture of a boy with spiky brown hair playing the guitar came up. "Lola, he's cute!" she cried.

Lola adjusted her cloth headband. "I told you," she mumbled.

STRIKER15: STICKS? U THERE?

"This is perfect." Andie continued, pointing to his Interests section. "See, it's all right here—soccer, chocolate milkshakes, snowboarding, ice hockey, the Great Lawn in Central Park, burgers from Corner Bistro—oh my God and he likes the Shins!" Andie's eyes lit up. "Tell him you're listening to *Wincing the Night Away.*"

"What?" Lola asked, confused.

"Just say exactly that!" Andie commanded, nudging Lola in the ribs. Lola typed the IM slowly, exactly the way Andie had said it.

LOLABEAN: LISTENING TO WINCING THE NIGHT AWAY
STRIKER15: U LIKE THE SHINS? I'M OBSESSED W/ KISSING THE LIPLESS.

"Ew." Lola cringed.

"No, Lola. It's a song—it's good. Tell him you love it too."

LOLABEAN: LOVE THAT SONG 2!

There was a long pause and Lola bit her lip, hoping Kyle wouldn't ask her another question. She felt like she had showed up for the hardest math quiz of the year without studying, and now she had to cheat off Andie.

STRIKER15: ☺

"It's working!" Lola clapped her hands in front of her face.

"See?" Andie said, smoothing back her bangs. "I told you! Ask him if he likes Iron & Wine—if he likes the Shins he's probably into them too." Lola straightened up and started typing faster on the keyboard.

LOLABEAN: DO U LIKE IRON & WINE?

STRIKER15: THEY'RE AWESOME.

LOLABEAN: I KNOW!!!!!!!

"Lola," Andie giggled, "try not to use so many exclamation marks."

Lola smiled. She would have used a million exclamation marks if she could have. She hadn't been this excited since she met J. K. Rowling at the Barnes & Noble in West London.

LOLABEAN: WANT TO HANG OUT THURSDAY?

Lola held her breath, waiting for Kyle's response.

STRIKER15: 4 SURE.

Lola let out a shriek and threw her thin arms around Andie, hugging her tight. "You're brilliant!" she cried. Tomorrow she'd do exactly what Andie had taught her—toss her hair, wear perfume, keep on about soccer and snowboarding and kissing the bloody lipless. And by the end of the day . . . well, maybe she'd be doing some kissing too. Hopefully not with the bloody lipless.

LET THEM EAT CAKE

It didn't matter that Stella was almost officially a New Yorker—today she felt like any other dim tourist. It was Wednesday afternoon and she was wandering around Soho, looking for the Greene Street Bakery. She was tired, hot, and sweaty. Two French girls stopped suddenly in front of the Prada window to look at the army of impeccably dressed mannequins. "*Magnifique!*" one cried, pointing at something inside. For the first time in her life, Stella saw the Prada logo and kept walking, like it was just another Ann Taylor Loft. It was almost five o'clock and she was on a mission.

Stella turned the corner and headed down Greene Street. Fire escapes hugged the wide beige buildings, and the cobblestone streets reminded her of Covent Garden in London. With a little luck she would get to the bakery before it closed. She imagined the girls lounging in Cate's room, laughing about Hailey Plick's nose job (the one she had gotten "to breathe better"). Stella gritted her teeth. This whole initiation thing was getting old, fast.

She had completed the first four "trials" after school yester-day. She'd had to run out to Jojo's on Sixty-fourth Street to pick up a warm asparagus salad, because Cate didn't want the lobster ravioli their chef, Greta, had made. And the list was multiply-ing faster than a mathlete at state championships. Today Stella had carried not only her books, but her massive Chanel makeup bag, meeting Cate after every other class so she could touch up her bronzer. After school Cate had requested ham-and-Gruyère sandwiches for when the Chi Beta Phis came over. Stella had asked if Greta could do it, but Cate had insisted she wanted a snack with a "more personal" touch. Now Stella was finally in Soho, a half an hour late for her meeting with some woman named Celine Kahn, someone who Cate had called "the Vera Wang of wedding cakes."

She got to the building with a minute to spare and knocked hard on the dark wood door. A young woman poked her head out and frowned.

"Sorry—we're closed," she said, then disappeared into the back. The door slammed shut.

Stella's heart raced. She'd done everything Cate asked her to, even acted like she was *happy* to garnish Cate's salad and hand-wash her delicates. But that was only because she knew that by Saturday she'd be *in*. But if she didn't bring back cake samples . . . it was all over. Forget doodling on Priya's notebook during lunch, forget sleepovers or brunch at the MoMA—it would be her, Myra Granberry, and Myra's mus-tache from now on.

She knocked determinedly on the door, over and over again,

until her knuckles hurt. Finally the woman opened it, her overly plucked eyebrows slanted into two harsh lines. Stella smiled sweetly. "I'm Stella Childs. I had an appointment with Celine for the Sloane-Childs wedding?" *You will do this,* Stella thought, trying to reach the woman's brain through osmosis. *You want to help me.*

The woman smoothed her hands over her apron, which was covered with so much flour it looked like she'd gotten caught in a snowstorm. "I'm Celine, but that appointment was half an hour ago. Why don't you give us a call tomorrow?" Celine started to close the door.

Stella let out a deep breath and rested her hand on the door before it shut, resigned to play the card that always won the game. "Well, that's a shame. My mum, *Emma*, is going to be disappointed." Stella watched Celine's face as she put the name together. *Emma* of the Sloane-*Childs* wedding. "She wanted the cake to be next to her in the *Vogue* spread—they're covering the wedding. I guess we'll just have to use another bakery. . . ."

Stella crossed her arms over her chest, waiting for Celine to cave. It wasn't a complete lie—even if V*ogue wasn't* covering the wedding, her mum *was* still Emma Childs.

"Let me see what I can do," Celine said finally. "I wouldn't want your mom to have to use someone else." Celine slowly stepped aside and opened the door.

Stella strolled into the bakery, its wide wooden tables covered with cakes that made Willy Wonka look like a slacker. One was dotted with red sugar roses so perfect and huge they looked like they were out of a Grimm's fairy tale. Another cake was shaped as a five-story fortress, surrounded by an electric blue moat of icing. A marzipan soldier was getting eaten by an alligator.

Stella breathed in the sweet cake batter smell and smiled. Today Greene Street Bakery—tomorrow Ashton Prep domination. Nothing could stop her now.

Cate sprawled out on her queen bed, her chin propped up in her hands. "How was the movie?" she asked, studying Priya's face.

"I told you—it was fine. Why are you so obsessed with the movie?" Priya shot Cate a curious look. Then she turned back to Cate's Mac, where she was clicking through her sister Veena's Flickr photos.

"I was thinking about seeing it," Cate lied. She stared into the open *Teen Vogue* in front of her, as if she was really interested in what Miley Cyrus's hairstylist had to say. Sophie and Priya had told her twice that they'd been at the Eighty-sixth Street movie house on Monday when she called. But Cate couldn't stop wondering if they were lying, and if Blythe had been with them. Blythe still hadn't told her where she'd gone after Barneys.

Cate closed the magazine and sat up on her bed. Blythe was sitting next to Sophie on the couch, taking her manicure off. Mini cotton balls covered in pale yellow polish were scattered on a tissue at her feet like popcorn. "So you're still not going to tell me where you ran off to the other day, are you?" Cate asked accusingly.

"I just can't," Blythe said, keeping her eyes on her pinkie nail. "Will you drop it—please?"

Sophie started humming, the way she always did when she wanted to fill awkward silences.

Cate sat back on her bed, annoyed. Blythe was definitely up to something. But maybe it didn't have anything to do with Priya and Sophie. Maybe she was hanging out with another group of girls. Madison Sheckner was a possibility—she had been jealous of Cate since fourth grade, when Cate got the lead in *Annie* over her. There was also Taylor McCourt. She had gone through an ugly-duckling-turned-swan transformation last summer, and had been building her group of friends ever since.

Sophie kept humming. It sounded like a strange medley of Rihanna and Josh Groban.

Cate gritted her teeth. "Quit it, Sophie," she snapped. Sophie glanced sideways at Blythe, who just shrugged.

"Doesn't Veena look so pretty in this picture?" Priya turned the laptop so Cate could see Veena at a Halloween party at Yale, dressed as a slutty cop. She glanced at Sophie, Blythe, and Cate, who were all silent. "What did you get at Barneys yesterday?" she asked, clearly trying to defrost the room.

"Well . . ." Cate replied slowly, her whole body perking up as she mentally recounted her purchases. "I got this top." She pointed to her white silk blouse.

"Theory?" Sophie asked, studying the cutouts along the neck.

"Precisely." Cate got up from her bed and disappeared into her closet. She emerged with two other hangers, one with a kelly green strapless dress, another with a canary yellow chiffon sleeveless blouse. She threw them across her bed for the girls to properly admire. She hadn't tried anything on at Barneys, but, like any seasoned shopper, she knew what styles and fabrics in each brand would work on her. (Lace-hemmed skirt from Nina Ricci? No, thank you! DVF wrap dress in bias-cut silk? Yes, please!)

Sophie walked over to the dress, gingerly touching its crisp hem. "Oh, I saw this on the Theory site—I love it!" she exclaimed.

"I told her she should wear the dress to the freshman banquet," Blythe chimed in from the couch. "It looks amazing with her skin." Cate looked at Blythe, pleased. Traitor or not, she was still the best at sucking up.

"I still have to get my outfit for that." Priya bit her lip.

Cate rested her hand on Priya's wrist. "You have to go to Searle—I saw a dress in the window and could just picture it on you. It was short, with red cap sleeves. Maybe we could all go in bright solids to make a statement."

Sophie nodded in agreement. "I already have a yellow Diane von Furstenberg dress I could wear—and Blythe, you could wear your blue Marc Jacobs dress. Loving it!" Sophie squealed, bouncing up and down on her kitten heels.

Cate tucked her dark brown hair behind her ear and imagined strolling into the drawing room at Ashton Prep, flanked by Priya, Blythe, and Sophie. Her lips curled into a satisfied smile. Everything was exactly how it was supposed to be: Cate was making the plans, and everyone else was following her lead.

Just then Stella strolled into Cate's room, her arms stacked with light pink and green bakery boxes. "I hope you're hungry!" she exclaimed. "I got extra sweets for us."

"I'm not really a dessert person," Cate said with a scrunch of her nose. "But thanks. You can put them over there." She pointed to the tiny antique coffee table in front of her couch.

Stella glared at Cate, resisting the urge to open a cake box and smush a piece right into her perfect pale face. She set the boxes down and Sophie, Blythe, and Priya swarmed the delicate, dollhouse-style table. Stella popped a box open.

"I'm a dessert person," Sophie cooed, closing her eyes. "They all smell so good."

Stella tucked a few curls behind her ears and pointed to the different cakes. "This is passion fruit for you, Priya. That's Harry's favorite flavor too—they had it at his New Year's Eve party, at the palace."

Priya leaned over the pink slice and smiled, impressed. "Are you talking about *Prince Harry?* You go to his New Year's Eve parties?"

"Of course—our fathers are friends." Stella smiled before moving onto the next cake. "That's coffee, coconut for you, Blythe, crushed vanilla bean, caramel for Sophie, and I got you hazelnut, Cate—but I guess I'll have to eat that myself." Stella picked up the small slice of hazelnut and took a bite, closing her eyes in delight.

Priya popped a bite of the passion fruit in her mouth, her dark eyes widening. "This is incredible!" she cried. She turned to Cate and mouthed, "I love her!" over her shoulder.

Cate plastered on her best fake smile, the one she'd used when her great-aunt Clara gave her a terrarium for her birthday.

Just then someone knocked on the door. "Come in!" Cate

cried. "Unless you're Lola or Andie," she mumbled under her breath. Priya laughed.

Winston walked into the room, running a hand through his thick graying hair. "Hi, girls," he said to the group, then looked past them to Cate. "Did you get those samples from the bakery?"

"Yes!" Stella called, passing the sealed box to Winston. "*These* are for you. The woman at the bakery said her favorite is passion fruit, with crème frosting—it would also look brilliant with the design mum picked."

Winston took the box out of Stella's hands and tilted his head. "Thank you, *Stella* . . ." He gave Cate a stern look. "Cate, can I talk to you for a minute?" He nodded toward the hallway. Cate narrowed her eyes at Stella.

Cate followed her dad into the hallway. Winston lifted the pale pink box in the air. "Cate—the cake samples were *your* responsibility."

She bit her lip. "But Daddy—I was busy."

Winston narrowed his eyes at her. "Busy hanging out with your friends?"

Cate ran her fingers along the wainscoting on the wall. "No . . . I did my bio homework too." She looked up at her father, waiting for him to soften. Last year she'd let the girls cut up all her dad's Zegna dress shirts to make one-of-a-kind outfits for the lower-school Bon Voyage Dance. Their *Project Runway*–esque efforts hadn't worked, but it had taken Cate only four minutes to talk her dad out of being angry.

Winston shook his head. "When I ask you to do something,

you do it—no dumping your responsibilities onto Stella. She has enough to deal with."

Why was he so concerned with Stella—what about *her*? "What does Stella have to *deal with*? Since she's been here, she's acted like a total princess," Cate spat angrily. Normally she never raised her voice to her dad, but she'd had enough. Not only was Stella brainwashing her friends, she was brainwashing her father too.

Winston's lips pressed into a hard line. "Cate, you don't know the half of it. The girls left London under . . . bad circumstances. Their father was having an affair, with some singer, Cloud Something."

"Cloud McClean?" Cate squeaked, the cheesy lyrics of "Kick It" spinning in her head. Cate had just seen Cloud McClean in this month's *Vanity Fair*, gushing about her twenty-third birthday party at EuroDisney and her new line of glitter thongs. The duke had run off with *her*?

Winston paused. "Please don't mention it—I shouldn't even have told you. But I hope now you'll be a little more . . . *gracious*. Emma and the girls have been through a lot this past year." He squeezed Cate's shoulders firmly, like he was sending her off on a humanitarian mission. Then he kissed her head and walked down the stairs.

She walked back into the room, her dad's words rolling around in her head. The girls were standing around Stella, who was bragging about all the elaborate balls she had been to at Buckingham Palace with her father, *the duke*. Now that Cate knew the whole story, she did feel badly for Stella. But she also knew the truth: that all Stella's talk about how "over" London was, and how fabulous her royal father was, were *all lies*. What else had she been lying about?

"Everything all right?" Stella asked, shooting Cate an innocent look. Cate dug her fingernails into her palm and glanced back and forth between Stella and Blythe. Stella was stabbing at a slice of cake in Priya's hand, and Blythe was sprawled out on the floor with Sophie, painting her toenails. Cate couldn't decide who was less trustworthy.

"Fine," she said cheerfully, offering Stella a sweet smile. Blythe was still a threat. So for now, she needed Stella in the group. But then again, so was Stella. . . .

TO: Blythe Finley, Priya Singh, Sophie Sachs
FROM: Cate Sloane
DATE: Wednesday, 9:18 p.m.
SUBJECT: RE: Democracy Now

Hi CBPs,

Just a friendly reminder re: the terms of Stella's trials. If she fails a single mission, it constitutes an overall failure, and her initiation process will be terminated immediately. Capisce?

Your prez,
Cate

THE MAGIC WORDS

Thursday afternoon, Andie and Lola stood across the street from Bryant Park. They watched as Lilianna Crosby, the actress who had adopted a child from almost every continent, strolled into the giant white tent, two babies crammed into a sack on her hip. Men in black IMG T-shirts guarded the entrance, spitting commands into their headsets as though they were trying to land a three-ton spacecraft in the middle of Fifth Avenue.

"I don't know about this," Andie said, pulling at the hem of her gray Zac Posen skirt. Today, while Emma and Winston had been busy drafting a seating chart with Gloria, Lola had suggested they sneak into the Alexander Wang show, to give Andie her first real taste of the fashion world. She'd found all the info in Emma's planner. It was a good idea—in theory—but they had no invites, no press passes, and they were at least ten years younger than everyone going inside.

"This is our chance!" Lola grabbed Andie's wrist and pulled

her across the street, nearly getting them flattened by a black Lincoln Town Car.

Andie and Lola snuck through the side entrance and ran into the tent, nearly colliding with a woman wearing a tiny hat that looked suspiciously like a dead hummingbird. They quickly disappeared into the crowd, squeezing through a group of people. They passed Curtis Harding, the lead singer of Demon Landlords, holding hands with a girl who looked like Tinkerbell. A German reporter pushed between them and shoved his press pass in Curtis's face. "Vat's next vor ze Demon Landlords?" he shouted.

Andie stared at the long white runway, awestruck. In the front row, a petite woman with wavy blond hair looked through her program. It was *Kate Moss*. Andie dug her fingers into Lola's arm. "This is unbelievable," she whispered. She'd waited years for the chance to be in the same room as her idol, and now she was just a few feet away. She breathed in deeply, hoping to soak up some of Kate's career karma.

Lola clapped her hands. "I told you!" she cried. They made their way toward the back of the room.

Arden Porsche, the New York City socialite notorious for her temper, argued with a woman with severe bangs. "Check your little chart again," Arden said, smacking the woman's clipboard. "I should be in the first row, not third—*first*."

Lola and Andie walked past white folding chairs filled with familiar faces. They hid in back of two model types standing behind the last row. One wore a striped jumper that made her look like a one-hundred-pound candy cane, the other a strategically ripped black T-shirt that barely covered her neon green bra.

"Have you heard anything about Alexander's collection?" the model in the jumper asked her friend.

"It's supposed to be inspired by her master bath. Think cold, stark, glossy," the girl with the ripped tee said importantly.

Andie scanned the room, her eyes falling on a woman sitting on the other side of the runway. Her hair was so long and thick it looked like she had a black blanket draped over her shoulders. "Lola!" Andie squealed, a little too loudly. "That's Ayana Bennington! She's one of the top agents in the world."

"I know—she's been trying to represent my mum for ages." Lola adjusted her headband. Andie had relented and let Lola wear a headband, but only if it was one of her choosing. She'd thrown the teal Duane Reade one in the kitchen trash (so Lola wouldn't be tempted to dig it out) and replaced it with one from Burberry. It wasn't a ten, but it'd do.

Andie straightened up and stood in Ayana's line of vision. It was only a matter of time before she noticed her. Andie would be her most successful client—the model who changed the industry, making "petite" the new "tall."

Just then Andie felt a tap on her shoulder. A man with long black hair and tortoiseshell-framed glasses stood behind them, chewing on the end of a pencil. His thin legs were packed into a tiny pair of black skinny jeans and his round belly hung slightly over his studded belt. He looked like an egg on toothpicks.

"Right, hi," he cooed, pointing the pencil at Andie, then Lola. "I assume you two escaped from the day care tent? Let me show you out—the show is about to start and I don't get paid nearly enough to babysit."

The model in the jumper let out a cackle. A few people in the back row turned around to see what the commotion was about. Andie's face flushed. This wasn't the kind of attention she wanted. "We, uh," she muttered, looking at Lola, who was wringing her hands nervously.

"Puh-lease," the man said, circling his pencil in the air. "I don't have time for little games from little people. Either I show you out or the police do." He turned and started for the exit.

Andie looked at the crowd in front of her. A couple across the runway glanced up from their programs. A woman in a full-length alpaca coat pointed. Andie stared at the back of Kate's head, hoping she wouldn't turn around. *WWKD?* But there was only one thing to do: make a graceful exit. Fast.

"Come on," Andie whispered, grabbing Lola's hand. "We need to go. *Now*." She tried to cover her face with her hair, like a criminal avoiding being seen on camera. Egg on Toothpicks was probably going to take her photo and e-mail it to Gawker.com, the snotty Manhattan media blog, with a note about the two clueless twelve-year-olds who thought they could sneak into Fashion Week. Forget modeling. Forget finding an agent. Andie Sloane was going to be blacklisted from the industry forever.

Lola stopped suddenly. "We can't leave," she said to Egg on Toothpicks's back. "I'm here for my mum—Emma Childs."

He turned around and pursed his lips coolly. He scanned Lola's gangly frame, his eyes stopping on her frizzy blond hair. "Emma Childs . . . *the supermodel*?" he asked snidely. Under his breath he mumbled, "And I'm Christy Turlington's hotter younger brother."

"Yes, Emma Childs *the supermodel*," Lola muttered. There was only one other Emma Childs—the bucktoothed host of *Sleeping with Simians*, an Animal Planet show about monkeys. She fumbled through her purse and found her wallet. She held out the picture of her and her mom on a yacht in Southwest France. "See?" she said, like it was her official pass into the show. "That's me and my mum. She couldn't make it, so she wanted us to come instead."

Egg on Toothpicks bit the pencil again. "Wait here."

He strode toward the runway and whispered to the woman with the clipboard. Then he returned, his face softer than before. "I'm so sorry for the miscommunication," he said apologetically, clasping his hands together as though he were praying. "I'm Anton Von Kleet. Let's get you two a little more . . . *situated*. Follow me." He walked through a narrow aisle. Lola grinned. Her mother's name always had magical powers.

They followed Anton toward the end of the runway, where Arden Porsche was sitting in the front row with a doughy friend. Arden's skirt was so tight her legs were turning blue. "Apologies, but we need these seats," Anton said breezily. He looked around the room as he spoke, as though Arden were a bear who'd maul him if he made direct eye contact. "We have something for you a few rows back."

Arden looked from Andie to Lola, her hand tightening around her plastic water bottle. "We're not going anywhere," she growled. With that, she emptied the contents of her water bottle onto Anton's alligator-skin boots.

Anton merely waved his hand in the air. Two burly security

guards immediately came over and pulled Arden and her friend flailing from their seats.

"Do you know who my father is?" Arden called over her shoulder as she was escorted out of the tent. "I will *ruin* you!"

"Ladies," Anton said calmly, gesturing to the two empty seats. "Let me know if you need anything. Evian, Pelligrino, perhaps?"

Andie shook her head and straightened up in her seat. Across the runway, Ayana Bennington and her assistant were standing up, trying to get a better look at the two twelve-year-olds who'd gotten Arden Porsche booted out of Fashion Week.

As the lights dimmed, Andie grabbed Lola's arm and squeezed. "This is incredible." Not only had they gotten inside, now they were VIPs. After the show they'd be eating caviar at the Bryant Park Hotel with Vivienne Westwood. And by next year's Fashion Week, Andie would be calling Dolce and Gabbana by their first names.

Lola looked around the crowd at all the famous faces. The thump of techno music filled the room and the first model stepped onto the runway in a white pleather evening gown. A hundred camera flashes went off. This *was* incredible. And if the magic words—Emma Childs—could get her into the front row at Fashion Week, then they could get her a lot of other places too. She looked at Andie, then at Ayana Bennington, who was whispering to the editor in chief of *Bazaar*, and got an idea. It was time to put her mom's name to the test.

TO: Ayana Bennington
FROM: Lola Childs
DATE: Thursday, 7:35 p.m.
SUBJECT: Future models

Dear Ayana Bennington,
Let me introduce myself. My name is Lola Childs and I am the daughter of Emma Childs (the supermodel—not the Animal Planet host). It was delightful to see you at the Alexander Wang show tonight! Like yourself, we were fortunate to get front-row seats.

I'm writing because my sister Andie and I would like to meet with you to discuss future careers in modeling. Do you have any time available this week? I know my mum would appreciate it (she's been so busy with wedding planning it's hard for her to find time to write).

Cheers,
Lola Childs, Esq.

TO: Lola Childs
FROM: Ayana Bennington
DATE: Friday, 8:58 a.m.
SUBJECT: RE: Future models

Hello Lola!

So good to hear from you. I've spoken to your mother a handful of times and have always been a huge admirer of her work. Do send her my fondest regards.

I'd love to meet with you and your sister. This week is a bit hectic with the shows, but I'll be in my office for a few hours on Saturday afternoon. Would you be able to stop by then, say four thirty? I very much look forward to meeting you.

All my best,
Ayana

EVERY QUEEN NEEDS A COURT

"Here we are." Cate stopped at the entrance to a majestic stone mansion on Seventy-seventh Street. A black Mercedes was parked in the half-circle driveway, the driver leaning out the window to clip his fingernails. He stopped when he spotted Cate and Stella in the rearview mirror.

"Is this a school?" Stella asked, as two boys in crisp blue button-downs and striped ties walked down the front steps. After last period, they had cut through Central Park to the Upper West Side, for her last trial before the vote on Saturday. Cate had told Stella it would be "challenging," but she hadn't said anything more. She was acting like some bad reality TV host, trying to create suspense by being unnecessarily mysterious.

"This is Haverford." Cate crossed her arms over her chest and smirked. "It's our brother school." She walked across the driveway and up the stone steps to the arched entranceway, Stella following. There was a carved stone crest on the wall next to the giant oak doors—two winged lions holding a shield.

They pushed into a two-story entrance hall. Two marble staircases wrapped around the upper floor and emptied out on either side of the room, which was decorated with blue-and-red banners announcing every minor accomplishment from the last thirty years. Cate took a left down a wide tiled hallway that was mostly empty, except for a few stray boys lingering after school. A short boy with a bowl haircut walked past, struggling against the weight of a massive yellow backpack. He looked back and forth between the girls as if witnessing an alien invasion.

"Where are we going?" Stella asked, an edge in her voice. She had been so busy with all of the trials—picking up Cate's dry cleaning, baking cupcakes and biscuits for Cate's Junior Honor Society bake sale—she had only called Vera Wang yesterday to make an appointment for the girls to try on bridesmaid dresses. She'd hoped this next trial would be easy. But nothing was ever easy with Cate.

"Oh, you'll see . . ." Cate singsonged, twisting her dark brown hair into a ponytail.

The girls walked in silence, until Cate finally stopped outside the gym. One of the doors was propped open and Stella could see the Haverford varsity basketball team practicing. It seemed like the boys were genetically engineered to play the sport—they were all at least five-foot eight, muscular, and adorable (maybe being adorable wasn't a requirement for playing basketball, but it sure made it more fun to watch).

"So this is your final trial," Cate told Stella, crossing her hands over her chest. Looking into Stella's big green eyes, she almost felt a little guilty. "If you do this, you're as good as in." Cate assumed

Stella would fail—and then Cate could show her generosity by forgiving her this one thing and letting her in anyway. That way Stella would be grateful and never forget her place in the order of the sisterhood.

Or if the girls voted her out . . . well that would provide its own karmic balance.

Stella looked back at the boys in the gym. A blonde in a T-shirt that read MAINE did a layup and the ball swooshed through the net. "Bring it," she said, leveling her eyes at Cate. She had been able to do everything so far—what was one more trial?

"See those shorts?" Cate continued, nodding toward the gymnasium. All of the boys were wearing blue shorts with a red stripe down the sides. On the front of each thigh was a printed number. "Those are the Haverford signature shorts. I need you to steal all fourteen pairs and bring them back to me by five thirty."

Cate bit her lip in excitement. The Haverford basketball team were state champions, and they acted like it. They hardly talked to anyone who wasn't on the team, and all the Ashton Prep upper-school girls had worn black last year the week Braden Penny-worth, Haverford's point guard, got a girlfriend. Cate wanted to incorporate the team's signature shorts into Chi Beta Phi's gym wardrobe. Everyone at Ashton would be so jealous.

"The ones they're wearing right now?" Stella gulped, trying to keep her voice steady. She imagined running around to each of the giant players, trying to pants them without their noticing.

Cate nodded. "Oh," she added, turning to leave, "I'll be at Jackson Hole with Priya, Sophie, and Blythe. Bring the shorts there . . . but don't bother coming if you don't have them." She looked Stella in the eye and smiled, then offered her a breezy little wave. "Good luck. I'm out like pointy-toe shoes." Then she strutted back down the empty stone hall and disappeared around the corner.

Inside, a basketball swished through the hoop and a few boys threw their arms up and cheered. What was she supposed to do? Sneak into the boys' locker room *Mission Impossible* style, with grappling hooks and ninja gear? Stella pulled out her iPhone and looked at the time. It was four o'clock—the team probably wouldn't be done practicing until five. Maybe she could try to buy fourteen pairs from the school store, if they even had one. Not likely. The gym echoed with the sound of squeaky shoes and the thump-thump-thump of the bouncing ball.

"Heads up!" a voice called. The basketball bounced off the glossy wood floor and came careening toward Stella's head.

"Bloody hell!" she screamed, catching the ball just before it pummeled her face. The entire team was frozen on the court, staring at her. "Hi," she said softly.

The tall blonde bloke, the one who had scored the layup, gestured for Stella to throw him the ball. She tried to do a chest pass, but it fell a little short. She suddenly wished she had paid attention during gym at Sherwood Academy in London, instead of making fun of Ms. Reed's hairy armpits with Pippa and Bridget.

A few boys laughed. "Can we help you?" the blond guy said. He hugged the ball to his chest.

"Um . . ." Stella muttered. A boy with shoulder-length black hair whispered something to his freckled teammate. "I'm here to try out for the team." She tossed her golden curls over her shoulder and shot them all her cutest, most flirtatious smile. The guys looked at each other and laughed. Maybe this trial wasn't impossible after all. She just needed some help from a few new mates. Fourteen, to be exact.

Jackson Hole was bustling with Ashton Prep upper-school girls. Cate, Priya, Sophie, and Blythe went there every Thursday after school and always sat at the same table in the corner, so they could survey the room. Amber Haan, one of the prettiest seniors, sat with her friends at a table by the window, staring dejectedly at their plain bowls of lettuce. Kimberly Berth, who'd started referring to herself as "Kimmy Kim" last year, maneuvered between tables, dropping fliers for the school mascot club she was starting.

Sophie picked through a pile of sweet potato fries, her retainer perched on the edge of her plate. "Who wants to dress up as a bobcat?" she asked, eyeing the flier. Priya was sitting next to her with one elbow on the table, her left hand shielding her eyes from the swirly mustard-ketchup mixture Sophie always made.

"Losers," Cate answered. She looked at her silver Tiffany Crown of Hearts watch and then out the wall of windows on the far side of the restaurant. It was ten after five, and Stella was still nowhere in sight. She leaned back in her seat and smiled. She couldn't feel badly about it—she had given Stella a fair chance, and Stella knew the rules. If she couldn't complete all the trials, she couldn't be in Chi Beta Phi.

"I'm having order remorse," Blythe moaned, looking down at her chicken-finger parmigiana sandwich. They had put too much pasta sauce on it and the bread was soggy and red. She leaned across the table and stole a bite of Priya's turkey club. "I have to run to the ladies' room," she said, grabbing her midnight blue Marc by Marc Jacobs bag. "Sophie, come with?"

Sophie popped her retainer back into her mouth and started to get up.

Cate scraped her nails along the sides of her wood chair. During English Blythe had texted Priya twice, then shut off her phone when Cate asked her what it was about. If Stella wasn't going to make it in the Chi Beta Phis, Cate would have to watch her own back—and she didn't have eyes on both sides of her head. She slid out of the table and followed Blythe. "No—*I'll* come with you," she snapped.

Blythe bit her lip. "Um . . . sure." She heaved her bag over her shoulder and headed toward the small wooden door marked LADIES. Cate trailed her to the back of the restaurant, edging between the tightly packed tables.

Cate squeezed into the tiny white bathroom and closed the door. The fluorescent light above them buzzed. "What were you going to say to Sophie?" she demanded.

"Nothing," Blythe said, looking confused. "I just needed her tampons." She combed her fingers through her dirty blond hair. "What's your deal?"

Cate crossed her arms over her chest, annoyed. "I should ask you the same thing." She needed to set B.B. straight: *Either you're second-in-command, or you're out.* She didn't want to boot Blythe, boobs or not, from the Chi Beta Phis. But if that was what it came down to, Cate would do it. She'd have to . . .

"I know what you're trying to do." Cate leaned against the bathroom door and reached for the knob, pressing the lock down with a menacing click.

"What are you talking about?" Blythe squeaked, her orange face looking a little paler than usual.

"That comment at the sleepover. The eye roll at lunch the other day. You're staging a coup."

"Um . . . are you serious?" Blythe shook her head. "I'm not staging . . . a *coup*."

"Right. Then where did you go after Barneys on Tuesday?" Cate demanded, tapping her Tory Burch flat impatiently on the floor. Cate had trusted Blythe ever since third grade. She'd been the only one brave enough to come to the house after her mom died and sit with her as she cried. She had even brought Cate a present: her stuffed bear Randolph. She wanted desperately to trust Blythe again, she did. But listening to her flounder was like watching the Home Shopping Network—Cate just wasn't buying it.

Blythe looked up at the ceiling and sighed. "I can't tell you," she said softly.

"Stop lying to me!" Cate cried. She shook her head and a strand of dark brown hair fell in her face. "You're phonier than a Canal Street handbag!"

"Fine!" Blythe snapped. She pulled her bag off the hook on the wall and started digging through it. "I wanted to wait until Sunday, but I guess I'll have to do this now, in the freaking Jackson Hole bathroom." She pushed a robin's egg blue box into Cate's hand, along with a balled-up piece of white satin ribbon.

Cate stared at the small black type that read TIFFANY & CO., suddenly quiet. This whole time Blythe was sneaking around . . . buying her presents?

"I wanted to surprise you . . ." Blythe mumbled, "At the wedding." Cate opened the box. Nestled in a velvet pouch was a tiny sterling silver locket. "I know it's hard for you with your dad getting remarried. And I know how you like to have something of your mom's with you all the time." Cate held the silver necklace up in front of her face. The oval locket had a tiny silver orchid etched on its front. It was beautiful. "I thought you could put a picture of your mom in it, and you could wear it all the time. See?" Blythe popped open the front of it. "Priya and Sophie helped me pick it out."

Cate looked at the locket, then back at Blythe. The same Blythe who'd stayed up all night with Cate, helping her rehearse her lines when she played Titania in *A Midsummer Night's Dream*. She'd sat in the front row with the script for all three performances, just in case Cate forgot her lines.

Cate felt a knot rising in the back of her throat. "Thank you, Blythe," she said softly, putting the locket around her neck. "It's perfect." She leaned over and hugged her friend tightly, tears welling in her eyes.

She had been so stupid. Blythe was the same loyal friend she always had been—just with a bigger chest.

"I'm sorry," Cate whispered into Blythe's ear. She stood back and wiped a tear from her eye. "It's silly—I got nervous you were tired of being so . . . behind the scenes. Like, in my shadow."

"No . . ." Blythe muttered. She smoothed down the front of her purple striped button-down.

Cate opened the bathroom door, relieved. Everything was back as it should be. But as she moved through the restaurant, she suddenly remembered that Stella was the one who had planted the seeds of suspicion. *You should watch your back,* she'd said.

Stella was the schemer. She'd tricked Cate, to try to get into the Chi Beta Phis.

Cate glanced at her watch. It was five twenty-five. When Stella walked through the door late and empty-handed, this would all be over. No generous pardon for failing her final trial. No nothing. They had to be sisters—but they didn't have to be friends.

Cate sat back down and Blythe sat next to her. All the plates were gone, but Sophie had ordered a milk shake and was using her straw like an eyedropper, feeding herself tiny strawberry sips. She stopped suddenly, her gaze resting on something behind Cate. Priya was looking out the window too, her brown eyes wide.

"What?" Cate finally asked, turning around in her seat.

"No way!" Sophie squealed.

Cate couldn't believe it either. Stella was strolling around the corner . . . *with the entire Haverford basketball team.* Tall, blond Braden Pennyworth was in front, then a boy with peach fuzz brown hair, followed by a kid who looked like Josh Hartnett's stunt double. Cate counted fourteen of them, and all of them were cute. She looked at her watch, hoping against hope that it was past five thirty.

But it was five twenty-nine.

Braden opened the glass door of the restaurant so Stella

could step through. Every head in Jackson Hole turned toward the doorway as Stella strutted confidently down the central aisle, the collar of her cherry red Lacoste polo shirt popped up. She approached the table, picking up the hem of her pleated uniform skirt and curtsying. "You said to bring back the shorts," she said smugly, her olive green eyes shining. "I hope it's okay that the team is still in them."

Cate gritted her teeth.

Priya eyed the Josh Hartnett look-alike. "It's definitely okay!" she cried, shooting him a little smile.

"Definitely . . ." Blythe pulled her shoulders back, sticking out her chest.

"Good." Stella kept her eyes on Cate. "This is Braden," she said, pointing to the blond boy, "and this is Ryan, Nate, Kevin, Drew . . ."

Cate stopped listening after the fifth name. She hated that *Stella* was introducing *her* to Braden Pennyworth. She might as well have been telling her what subway to take to Union Square, or recommending the pumpkin waffles at Sarabeth's.

The boys crowded around the table. Blythe was talking to five of them at the same time, telling them about her summer in Greece. Sophie and Priya stood up to talk to Braden, whose biceps were perfectly toned, as though all he did was eat, sleep, and play basketball. Cate stayed in her seat, feeling like she might puke up her tuna melt.

She squinted her eyes, trying to pretend the boys were the Haverford chess club, and Braden Pennyworth was just Fillmore Weitz, the four-foot-nine pizza-faced eighth-grader who'd actually had the nerve to ask her to the Haverford formal last year. But it was useless. Braden Pennyworth was still Braden Pennyworth, and Stella was still blond, gorgeous, and determined to weasel her way into the Chi Beta Phis.

When all the boys had filed out the glass door, Stella pulled up a chair and sat down at the end of the table—the *head* of the table. She had done it: completed the final trial, on time, and given the girls a much-needed dose of hotness. She was as good as in.

"Omigodomigodomigod!" Sophie cried, pressing her hands to her face. "I cannot believe that just happened."

Priya kept gawking at Stella like she was a celebrity. "How'd you do that?" she asked, twisting her shiny black hair into a ponytail.

"Did you see the boy with the moppy hair?" Blythe breathed. "Drew? I touched his six-pack."

Cate cleared her throat. "You know, technically the trial was to *steal* the shorts," she pointed out. "If I order filet mignon, I can't accept Spam."

Priya grabbed Sophie's milk shake and took a sip. "What are you talking about? I would much rather meet fourteen Haverford guys than sift through a pile of smelly gym shorts," she laughed.

"We *never* hang out with guys," Blythe agreed.

Cate looked down at the beat-up wood table, a little hurt. Fine, Cate had never set up any Haverford meet-and-greets, but had they forgotten about last spring, when she'd held a sleepover at the W hotel penthouse? Or the time she'd hired a driver to take them to East Hampton for the day, where they ate oysters at Della Femina, next to Natalie Portman?

"Forget waiting until Saturday to vote," Priya added, "I think Stella should be in." Stella straightened up in her chair, looking pleased.

"But I specifically said *steal*," Cate said desperately. She looked around for support, but Blythe and Sophie were staring at the table, staying Switzerland-neutral. "Fine, let's vote then," she growled. She stared at Sophie, who was carving an S into the table with her fork. "Who wants Stella to be in?"

Priya and Blythe looked at Stella and slowly raised their hands.

Sophie was still working at her S. "I don't want to vote," she said nervously, shaking her head. Ever since sixth grade, when Sophie joined the sorority, she had always voted with Cate—always.

"You have to," all four girls said at the same time.

"Fine." Sophie put down her fork, then slowly raised her hand. "I think Stella should be in," she said, cringing.

Cate let out a deep breath.

"Fine," Cate sighed, defeated. "You're in." She leaned back and crossed her arms.

"Cheers!" Stella cried. She clasped Priya's hand, overjoyed. Now that she was an official member, it was only a matter of time before she was telling Sophie which pair of sandals she should wear with her teal Cynthia Rowley dress, or telling Blythe to stop using so much bronzer. Stella never had been good at following orders—but giving them? That was something she excelled at.

"We should go to the Pierre to have tea Saturday to celebrate—it's supposed to be just like the Ritz," she said confidently.

"Let's do it," Priya agreed.

Cate shook her head, seething. Stella had made it into the Chi Beta Phis and now she was stuck with her—forever. Every sleepover, every sample sale, every Sunday afternoon in Sheep Meadow—Stella would be there, hanging out with *her* friends. And once someone was voted in, they were in. It was practically impossible to get them out.

Or was it?

Suddenly Cate remembered the day after *Finding Nemo on Ice*, when she took the Nemo hat Beth Ann Pinchowski had bought her and gave it to Sophie's dog Peanut to use as a chew toy. Beth Ann had stormed out of Sophie's room and stopped talking to them completely. She'd become friends with Tabitha Ferguson, a mousy girl with a gap between her front teeth.

Cate pulled her iPhone out of her purse and held it up to Sophie. "Sophie," she said loudly, waving her phone in the air. "Can you help me pick out a new ring tone?"

Stella was describing Braden Pennyworth's cologne—something between Old Spice and Drakkar Noir. Sophie turned away from the conversation and pushed a flat piece of light brown hair out of her eyes.

"What?" she asked, a little annoyed.

"I need a new ring tone—I was thinking of using that new song, 'Kick It'? By *Cloud McClean*? You know who she is, right, Stella?" Cate raised her eyebrows suggestively.

Stella stopped talking, her face ashen. Her face looked confused, then betrayed, as though Cate had taken a picture of her picking her nose and sent it to every newspaper in London. Cate felt the slightest pang of guilt. That *was* sort of hitting below the belt. But lying and friend-stealing were equally bad crimes.

"You are not using that song," Priya said, whipping her head around. The jeweled stud in her nose caught the light. "She wears *unitards.*"

Stella sat up straight in her seat and cleared her throat. She wanted to crawl under the table and cry, but she would never give Cate that satisfaction. "Don't you guys vote for the leader every year?"

Blythe, Priya, and Sophie all looked at each other, then at Cate. "Um . . . yeah, technically." Priya let out a nervous laugh. Sophie rested her chin on her hand and started humming softly.

"We should have a revote," Stella pressed on, glancing around at the girls. She looked directly at Cate and smirked. She didn't know how Cate had found out about the affair, but that comment was just cruel. And cruelty deserved retaliation.

"That's a good idea," Blythe agreed, tucking her hair behind her ears. "It is a new year . . . and we *are* in the upper school now."

Cate dug her nails into her palm. Blythe was agreeing to this? She must've been angry about the interrogation in the bathroom. None of them were thinking straight—did they really want some random British girl bossing them around? They'd be drinking tea every Saturday for the next four years, their teeth slowly turning a dull yellow.

Priya tilted her head from one side to the other. "Yeah, let's do it," she said. Sophie nodded slowly in agreement.

"Brilliant," Stella cried, clasping her hands together and grinning. "Then it's settled. We can vote at the Pierre on Saturday." She shot Cate a sweet smile.

Cate clenched her fists. Stella was out for her throne. Now it was *really* on.

WINNING PRINCE CHARMING

ola leaned in close to Elton John's shiny face, studying the gap between his teeth. "He looks so real," she said softly.

"I thought you went to the one in London." Kyle pushed his bangs off his forehead. He walked past a wax figure of Tina Turner and touched her hair. She looked like she'd been attacked by a crimping iron.

They'd decided to go to Madame Tussauds tonight, while Kyle's parents went to see a new off-off-Broadway play where a man disassembled a television set while singing opera.

"No, never," Lola said, staring at Kyle for a second too long.

Since her "lesson" on Tuesday, Lola had been studying nonstop—tossing her hair in the mirror and walking down the sidewalk so carefully an old lady with a walker had passed her. She'd even memorized the Wikipedia article on football (er, soccer) word for word and knew all the field positions (goalie, fullback, forward, midfielder). She was ready.

Kyle sniffed the air like a dog trying to pick up a scent. "I keep smelling vanilla cake batter in here," he said. "Weird."

"That's just my perfume," Lola said softly, tossing her hair over her shoulder flirtatiously, the way Andie had shown her. She had on her favorite pair of Gap jeans, the only ones that actually came down past her ankles, and one of Stella's "casual tops"—a bright green silk blouse. This morning had been better than Christmas. She'd discovered Stella's missing boxes under her bed—DRESS TOPS III and BEAUTY SUPPLIES—just in time for her date. She was considering them payment for Stella hanging out with Cate all week.

"Since when do you wear perfume?" Kyle asked, furrowing his eyebrows. Next to them, three older boys with Mahwah High sweatshirts tried to look up Tina Turner's sequined skirt.

"Since always," Lola said, turning away quickly. Her face felt hot and red. She felt a little silly acting, but it seemed to be working. Kyle had already complimented her once on her shirt, telling her she looked so . . . *girly*. He hadn't mentioned the ice cream disaster, either. It was like he had selective amnesia, forgetting only the things Lola wanted him to.

"Look!" she cried, spotting a few familiar friends. "The Spice Girls!" Scary Spice was sticking out her tongue, showing off a silver stud. Victoria Beckham was crouched down in Posh Spice mode, her arms raised above her head. Lola smiled, seeing an opportunity. "I wish I got to see Becks play when he was on Manchester United."

"Totally," Kyle agreed, resting his hands on the waist of his mesh shorts. "Wait . . ." He paused. "You never told me you liked soccer. Or do you just like Beckham?"

Lola stared into Kyle's big brown eyes and then shoved his shoulder playfully, just like she'd rehearsed with Andie. "I love football," she lied. "It's my favorite sport—right after snowboarding."

"You snowboard?" Kyle smiled at Lola, revealing his dimples. A church group in blinding fluorescent yellow T-shirts strolled through, pausing to take pictures with Miley and Billy Ray Cyrus. "Impressive."

Lola's whole body warmed up. "Cheers." She smiled, walking alongside him into the Hall of Presidents.

Lola stood next to Kyle, staring at a man with a nose so big it needed its own zip code. The rehearsal dinner was Saturday night, and her mum had told her she could bring anyone she wanted. Stella and Cate were bringing those daft girls who were always at the house, and Andie had said she'd probably bring Cindy. But Lola only had one person in mind. Her palms started to sweat just thinking about it.

"Do you know who any of these people are?" Kyle asked, glancing at a white-haired man with a saggy neck and a Will Smith look-alike. They were standing behind debate podiums in one corner of the room.

Lola laughed. "I don't have a bloody clue." She could stare at the big-nosed man all day long and she still wouldn't know.

"Well, this is Richard Nixon—we learned about him in history class." Kyle pulled his gum out of his mouth and pinched it between his fingers, a mischievous grin curling over his lips. "Dare me to stick some gum up his nose?"

"No!" Lola squealed, swatting him in the arm. She glanced

around the hall, but the tourists had disappeared. There was only a middle-aged man in a tracksuit muttering furiously to "Bill Clinton."

"Oh, come on. Remember when we used my mom's hair dryer to melt all those crayons?" Kyle grinned wickedly, and Lola smiled too. Growing up, she and Kyle were always doing things they weren't supposed to—using the buds of his mum's rhododendrons as ammunition in their fort war, mixing Stella's different creams to make a "potion." She'd never had so much fun breaking the rules.

"Fine," Lola said softly. "I *dare* you." She put her hands on her hips. Kyle looked both ways before stuffing the wad of blue gum up Nixon's big nose. Lola clapped her hands in front of her face and laughed.

"We have to get out of here—fast," Kyle said, grabbing Lola's thin arm. He pulled her toward the Hall of Sports Figures, the two of them erupting in a fit of giggles.

Lola ran toward the glowing red EXIT sign, feeling happier than she had since she'd arrived in New York. Kyle was already forgetting his old mate Sticks—the one who had terrible bangs and wore board shorts over her bathing suit when they went swimming in his pool in London.

Lola caught her reflection in the mirrored doors, her kelly green silk top looking perfect with her pale freckled skin. She was already forgetting Sticks too.

BALL GOWNS AND BLOWOUTS

Stella rested her hand on the cold metal clothing rack. It was packed with bridesmaid dresses, a cloth rainbow of greens, purples, browns, and blues. "So we should each pick a different style, but we'll all do satin and we'll all be in the same color— apple green," she said authoritatively, pinching a pale green dress between her fingers. She'd picked the color out of a French *Vogue* wedding spread.

Lola and Andie sat on the beige settee, quietly nodding. Cate was texting furiously on her mobile. She hadn't taken her Prada sunglasses off since they left the town house, not even when they entered the soft lighting of the Vera Wang dressing suite. Emma stood on a pedestal in the middle of the room as Gloria tucked her fingers into the sweetheart neckline of her dress, pulling it up.

Cate dropped her iPhone into her black Prada Cervo pleat bag. "Sophie says hi," she said breezily, picking up an armful of dresses without even looking at them.

Stella gripped the metal rack tighter. "That's funny, I just talked to her." Cate had been trying to taunt her all day—bragging about how she and Priya had run around the Central Park reservoir during gym, or how Sophie had said the *funniest* thing in geometry. But Stella hadn't flinched. She'd been texting all day with Blythe and Priya, and she had talked to Sophie online after school. They kept asking her about the Haverford basketball team and when they were going to hang out with them again. Stella had promised something was "in the works," but she hadn't talked to the boys since yesterday. And she wouldn't . . . not until the girls voted her their leader.

Cate picked up the skirt of one of the pale green dresses and scrunched up her nose. "Ugh. *Of course* you picked this color. I'm going to look so washed out." She strutted into the dressing room, slamming the oak door shut.

Andie and Lola began thumbing through the rack like they were in slow motion, every now and then pulling out a dress only to put it right back. Gloria fanned out the small train of Emma's gown. Her gold bracelets clinked together, making a sound like wind chimes. When Gloria had told Vera Wang *Emma Childs* was getting married—this Sunday—she'd offered one of her couture gowns as a wedding present.

"I adore this floral waist corsage—breathtaking," Gloria cooed, pressing her fingers to the fabric on the side of the dress. It was delicately formed into roselike flowers. Stella had already oohed and aahed over the mermaid dress. It could have been covered in rubies and diamonds—it didn't change the fact that her mum was getting married this Sunday and stranding them, permanently, in New York.

Lola pulled a bubble-hem satin gown off the rack and held it up to her lanky frame. "This is gorgeous!" she cried.

"That wouldn't look right on you," Stella said, taking the hanger from her. She picked out a full-length strapless dress with an empire waist and shoved it in Lola's arms. "This one's for you, and this," she said, passing the short dress to Andie, "is for *you.*"

"Thanks, Stella!" Andie said brightly, hugging the dress to her chest. Then she retreated to the dressing room.

"Cheers," Lola mumbled. Lately her self-confidence had been on a roller coaster. She'd felt good yesterday, pretty, even, hanging out with Kyle. But suddenly she felt like the ugly duckling again. She couldn't help but remember the way that man with the skinny little legs at Fashion Week had looked at her at first— like he couldn't *believe* she was Emma's daughter. Lola turned the dress over in her hands and looked at her mom, who was studying her reflection in the mirror. Sometimes Lola couldn't believe it either.

Stella turned back to the rack and her gaze fell on another full-length satin dress with a deep V-neck in the front and the back. With the exception of the pale green color, which screamed *Wedding!*, it was just the kind of dress she would wear.

She pulled off her red gingham halter and slipped the soft satin dress over her head. It clung perfectly to every curve—not that Stella had much in that department, but it emphasized what was there. She'd pair it with her silver Manolo Blahniks with the brooch on the toe and twist her curly hair up, a few tendrils falling in front of her face. A diamond solitaire in each ear would be the finishing touch. She stared at her reflection and smiled.

"Mum!" she called, opening the door of the dressing room. Gloria and Emma looked up from studying the Chantilly lace detailing on the front of the wedding dress. It reminded Stella of the curtains in her grandmother's sitting room.

"Nice," Gloria said flatly, then went back to Emma's dress, fluffing the small train. Her face was stiff and expressionless, like it had been blasted with liquid nitrogen.

"It's lovely, Stella." Emma pushed a blond tendril away from her face.

Lola stumbled out of the dressing room in her strapless gown, her jeans still twisted around one ankle. She hopped on one foot, kicking furiously as if a denim boa constrictor had grabbed hold of her leg. The top of the dress sagged at her chest, and the criss-crossing tan lines on her back made it look like she was wearing a white Speedo.

"No, no, no." Gloria ran her mauve fingernails through her thin hair. "We need to cover up those tan lines. And you'd need a padded bra."

Emma pressed two fingers to her lips. "Let's try something else, luv," she said, offering Lola a weak smile.

Andie emerged from the dressing room wearing the bubble-hem dress that Stella had picked out for her. The style was perfect. She looked like a pale green bell. "What do you think?" she asked, biting her lip nervously.

"You look like quite the young lady," Emma cooed.

"Thanks, Emma!" Andie cried, her face turning a pleased pink. She spun around twice, admiring herself in the mirror, then returned to her dressing room.

Stella watched as Lola adjusted her Burberry headband, the nose twitch just barely visible. "Come on," she said. "I'll help you find something else." They returned to the rack and started thumbing through it again as Gloria and Emma disappeared into the wide curtained dressing room designed especially for brides.

The door to Cate's dressing room swung open and she strutted out, a pleased grin on her face. She had twisted her dark brown hair up into a sleek bun, and she was wearing a full-length gown with a deep V-neck in the front and in the back. It was a beautiful dress. It was also the same one Stella was wearing.

"Too late," Stella snapped.

Cate scanned Stella's outfit, then rested her hands on her hips. "What do you mean, 'too late'?" she asked indignantly. "This dress looks amazing on me."

"Well, I've already decided I'm wearing it." Stella stepped toward the full-length mirror on the wall, annoyed. It was shopping 101—first to try is first to buy.

"No, you're not—it fits me perfectly." Cate followed Stella to the mirror and stood behind her, talking over her shoulder at her reflection.

Stella met Cate's gaze in the mirror. "I'd rather snap the heels off my Louboutins than let you wear it," she said coolly, turning to the side to see her profile.

"Lola!" Cate cried, spinning around. Lola froze, one hand on the dressing room door. "Who looks better in this dress—me or Stella?" Cate demanded.

Stella rested her hands on her hips and raised her eyebrows

as if to say, *You already know the answer to this question.* Stella was the one who had taken care of Heath Bar when Lola was at equestrian camp last summer—she had even let the little furball sleep on her pillow!

"Um . . . right," Lola bit her finger and looked back and forth between the girls, her skin second-degree-sunburn red.

"Lola, it's a simple question—who looks better in it?" Stella kept her eyes on Lola. Fine, she hadn't spent the last week French-braiding Lola's hair, but she was still her *sister*.

Just then, Gloria pulled the curtain open and Emma stepped out. She had changed back into her bright yellow dress with thick rope halter straps. Gloria passed Emma her black heels while arguing with her mobile. "You will never work again!" she threatened, staring menacingly at the glossy screen.

"Forget it," Cate growled. "I'm wearing it. I'm the head of Chi Beta Phi and I've decided I want this dress—you *have* to listen to me."

"No way," Stella cried. "We're having a revote tomorrow. You're not going to be in power for long." Soon Cate would be carrying *her* books.

Emma sat down on the small beige couch and eyed the girls. "Stella," Emma said in a calm but serious voice, "it's not a big deal. Just pick another dress."

"Mum!" Stella squealed, spinning around. "I tried this on first!" But Emma shot her a look that said, *That wasn't a question.*

Stella was about to head back into the dressing room but thought better of it. She pulled up the hem of her long gown, holding up one silver Sigerson Morrison wedge for Cate to see.

"Like my shoes?" she whispered. "Blythe lent them to me." Blythe had pulled her aside after Jackson Hole and told her what a great idea the revote was.

Cate slapped her palms to her cheeks in mock surprise. "I *thought* I recognized those," she cried. "Her senile golden retriever peed on them last year. She swore she'd never wear them again." Cate leaned forward so that she was close to Stella's ear. "They're rejects—*just like you.*" Stella retreated to her dressing room, slamming the door shut.

Cate grinned. So it was a lie; Blythe had never even had a dog. But Cate was like the NASA space station—it was dangerous to push her buttons. She twirled around in the mirror and looked at the dress one last time. It *did* look better on her. Forget the wedding. She'd wear it Saturday, for her victory lap around the town house.

A LITTLE BRIBERY NEVER HURT ANYONE. . . .

Cate tapped on the dressing room door with her midnight blue nails like she was playing "Chopsticks."

"Sophie," she singsonged. "Come out, I wanna see."

She spun around, surveying the Marc Jacobs flagship store. A wall of purses stood in front of her, with more varieties than a midtown deli's all-you-can-eat buffet. She breathed in, loving the rich, leathery smell.

This morning had been like some sort of sick Upper East Side torture. First Cate had woken up to find Lola's creature vomiting fur pâté on her new Jimmy Choos. Then Stella had decided to go all sugar mama and take the group to Pastis for brunch, putting it on her AmEx gold card. Sophie and Priya had gone on for twenty minutes about how good the brioche French toast was—Stella's recommendation. They'd even tried to feed some to Cate, who had insisted (for the ten thousandth time!) that she hated sweets. Cate had spent most of the meal pushing her eggs

Norwegian around on her plate, determining just how she was going to top Stella's brunch.

She wasn't above bribing the girls, especially now that the pressure was on: The vote was today, at four o'clock. Cate had decided to take everyone shopping at the Marc Jacobs store in Soho. Cate and Stella had each asked Emma and Winston for a plus-one-and-a-half, so they could bring all the Chi Beta Phis to the wedding. Now they were picking out new dresses—*on Cate*. Who needed brioche French toast when you could have a gorgeous silk gown?

Sophie crept out of the dressing room in a short cocktail dress. The pink satin made her look like a giant slab of grilled salmon. She spun around once and squealed. "You look fabulous," Cate pronounced. The color clashed with the rosy undertones in Sophie's skin, but Cate wasn't going to obsess over *minor* details. Sophie patted down her pin-straight light brown hair and smiled at her reflection.

"I don't know," Stella said, strolling along the long rack of clothes, her two fingers walking along the fabrics. "Salmon feels a bit last season." She scrunched up her nose like she'd caught a whiff of rotting fish.

"Not at all," Cate said sharply, shooting Stella a dirty look. "*Metallics* were last season—salmon is in. Trust me, Sophie."

Sophie looked at her reflection in the mirror behind the sales counter, her face twisted with worry. "Let me try something else on," she mumbled, retreating into the dressing room.

Cate spun around and glared at Stella, her fists clenched tight. "Stop trying to sabotage me," she growled.

Stella rested her hand on her heart, like a real American pledging allegiance. "What? I was just helping out a friend in fashion need." She smiled sweetly, then sat down on one of the cream-colored leather couches and daintily crossed her legs.

Blythe ran out of the dressing room toward Cate. "This is the one," she shrieked. A black checked fabric stretched over her new curves.

Priya trailed behind her in a pale pink shift dress with classic lines. "O.O.C.," she cooed, running her fingers over the glittery jewels embroidered into the fabric. She'd started abbreviating "out of control" back in seventh grade, but it still hadn't caught on.

Stella eyed Blythe's dress, crossing her arms over her chest. "It doesn't do anything for your figure," she said, shaking her head. "You want something that shows off your two new mates."

"Are you kidding?" Priya asked. "That dress is *all* boobs." Blythe admired her profile in the mirror.

Cate clasped her hands together happily and glanced at Stella. She was biting her lip dejectedly like someone had just thrown up a five-course meal in her Gucci Positano bag.

Priya twirled around. "On behalf of my closet—thank you," she cried, pulling Cate into a hug.

Sophie came out of the dressing room in a strapless navy blue cocktail dress with gold lamé polka dots. "Thanks, Cate," she seconded, leaning over to join the hug.

Stella picked up her Gucci bag and slung it over her shoulder. "I need some air," she muttered. She walked past the long table of shoes and sweaters, and out the massive black door to Mercer Street.

"What's with her?" Blythe asked, not taking her eyes off her own reflection.

"She's just jealous," Cate replied, watching smugly as Stella, the green-eyed monster, disappeared down the street. The girls loved their dresses, and they loved Cate more than ever. Stella didn't have a chance.

Stella dropped her iPhone in her brown leather bag and strode confidently back into the Marc Jacobs store, a man in a cropped pin-striped suit following close behind her. She walked past the racks of gowns, the cool air goose-bumping her skin. Blythe had a shoe box under her arm and Sophie was trying on a pair of red open-toe pumps. Cate and Priya were browsing the wall of bags, examining a neon blue clutch.

Stella stopped in front of them and cleared her throat. "Are you guys done with your *off-the-rack* shopping?" She glanced around disgustedly, as though she had just walked into a Salvation Army. "If you are, we should all go upstairs to Marc's private showroom." Stella smoothed down the skirt of her tan sateen shirtdress, waiting for the girls to process what she'd just said.

"What?" Sophie cried, dropping a red pump on the floor.

"You're kidding." Blythe squeezed the shoe box to her chest.

"Girls—meet Gerard, *Marc's* personal assistant." Stella stared at Cate, whose face was flushed in anger. "My mum has been close with Marc forever—we went on holiday with him three years ago. He still plays tennis with my father when he's in London."

"I thought your dad lived in Sydney now?" Sophie asked, tilting her head to the side. Stella bit her lip, feeling Cate's eyes on her. Yesterday Priya and Sophie had asked her what her father was doing. She couldn't say what she was really thinking—*Cloud McClean*—so she'd continued her lies and said he'd gotten a job in Sydney, and was buying Stella her very own condo overlooking Darling Harbor.

Gerard tucked his BlackBerry into the front pocket of his suit jacket, which looked like it had been shrunken in the dryer—the sleeves revealed six inches of tanned, waxed forearm. "Follow me, dolls. Marc just finished next season's collection." He turned and started toward the front of the store, Stella and the girls following close behind. Sophie looked over her shoulder at Cate, shooting her a look to say, *Sorry . . . but it's the new Marc Jacobs line. I'd shave my head to see this.*

Cate's head spun. The neon handbags seemed too bright, the fluorescent spotlights blaring. She bit her cuticle and looked at her Tiffany watch. There was only an hour and a half until tea at the Pierre. Stella had seen her Marc Jacobs dresses and raised her a designer collection.

As the girls followed *Marc*'s assistant up a narrow white staircase, Cate crept up behind them. Stella was a total mole, sneaking around and plotting against her, but Cate still had to see the new line.

The stairs emptied out into a wide room with stark white walls and high white tin ceilings. Light flooded in from the wall of windows, giving the room an almost holy glow, as if the girls had died and gone to designer heaven. A few headless mannequins were lined up in a row against the wall, a long rack of clothes next to them.

Gerard stopped in front of the first two mannequins. One wore a pale pink silk dress that resembled a nightgown, another a strapless floral dress paired with a structured military-style jacket in a crisp white. Sophie touched the silk fabric and smiled.

"Fabulous, yes?" Gerard cooed. "For his new spring collection Marc was playing with the idea of this youthful, angelic army. He's using a muted color palette of pale pinks, beiges, blues, and grays mixed with black and white. Take a look around and let me know what you'd like to try on." He made his way past the row of mannequins and brushed lint off one's shoulder, resting his hand on its boob to hold it steady. Then he pulled out his BlackBerry and started typing furiously.

Priya rested her hands on the mannequin's neck stump and turned to Stella. "Veena is going to be *so* jealous when I tell her what I did today. Actually, I'm going to make her jealous *right now*." She took out her iPhone and snapped a picture of the dress, sending it to her sister.

"I don't think you should try those on." Cate tried to sound convincing. "They look so fragile. . . . If you rip them you're going to owe Marc Jacobs, like, a million dollars." Cate knew that reason was lamer than BeDazzled Converse All Stars, but she was desperate.

Blythe turned away from a pale blue cotton dress with black zippers up each side, which looked too punk rock, like it could be accessorized with a studded dog collar. "Have you been sniffing glue with Myra Granberry? Who cares?" Blythe grabbed

Priya's arm and walked down the row of mannequins, pausing to admire each outfit. She leaned over and whispered something in Priya's ear.

"But there aren't even any dressing rooms!" Cate called at their backs.

"I don't think that's going to stop anyone." Stella smiled sweetly. She was standing across from the mannequins, thumbing through a rack of clothes. "And anyway, it's not like Gerard fancies us." Cate glanced across the loft space at Gerard, who was now leaning against the back wall, filing his nails with an emery board. Stella chose a hanger with a bubble gum–colored organza dress and walked confidently toward him.

Cate stared at the rack of clothes, torn. Sophie was thumbing through it, slinging dresses over her arm like she was looting the place.

"Cate!" she squealed, holding up a blue-and-white striped corset dress. "This would look great on you!" Cate studied it, then glanced across the room at Stella, who was talking to Gerard. Cate loved corset dresses, but she couldn't bear to let Stella know she was enjoying herself.

"Fine," Cate agreed. "But only because I don't want Marc Jacobs to think I'm rude." She tried hard not to smile as she strolled to the corner and pulled off her Anna Sui ruffle dress.

Across the room, Priya had tried on the strapless floral dress from the mannequin. "You could totally be a Marc Jacobs model," Blythe cried, fawning over her.

Cate zipped up the corset dress and walked over to the mirror. It looked amazing with her deep blue eyes and dark brown hair.

Stella slinked over. "You know you love it," she purred, eyeing Cate's dress.

"I'm actually a little disappointed," Cate said sharply, keeping her eyes on her reflection. "This collection is kind of bland. I guess I just have more sophisticated taste than you," she shrugged.

"Right, right." Stella laughed, rolling her eyes. She floated across the room in her pink couture gown. "You guys look amazing!" she called to Sophie and Blythe. They were huddled in a corner of the room, admiring their dresses.

With every compliment, with every smile, with every passing minute Stella was getting closer to the vote. And closer to the end of Cate's reign.

ANDIE AND THE BEANSTALK

Saturday afternoon, Andie stood in the mirrored elevator of Ford Models beside Lola, dragging her Kate Spade wedge heels across the red carpeting. Her hands shook as she stared at the buttons, and she felt like she'd downed fifty cans of Diet Coke. Number five glowed, then six. Just eight more floors to go.

She'd looked at the Ford Models website almost every day for the last year, and now she was here, minutes away from meeting with Ayana Bennington. She'd dreamed about being represented by Ayana—the same agent who represented Kate Moss, Heidi Klum, and Tyra Banks. Ayana was said to take on only three new models a year—if she agreed to represent you, you were destined for high fashion.

Andie smoothed down her skirt. She'd spent all morning figuring out what to wear, finally settling on a sleeveless blue Juicy Couture dress with crocheting down the front. She almost always wore her hair in a ponytail or a bun, but today she'd blow-dried it. It was shinier and smoother than Frédéric Fekkai extensions.

Lola clapped her hands together lightly. "You're going to be famous." Since the Fashion Week show, Lola had dubbed herself Andie's "manager" and was taking her duties very seriously. She even insisted on wearing a "power suit" to seem "professional," but it was really just a black skirt and a cropped Juicy jacket she'd stolen from Stella.

"I hope so," Andie murmured. Her heart beat faster and faster as the elevator hit the twelfth floor. She imagined Ayana Bennington, former-model-turned-agent, in a corner office overlooking Fifth Avenue. She'd hold Andie's face between her palms and just stare at it, falling hopelessly in love with every feature. Then she'd apologize for the trouble Andie had had with the website, for the fact that people hadn't seen her photo and called her immediately. *Idiots!* Ayana would cry. *Fools!* She'd slide a contract across the desk. *Welcome to Ford Models, Andie Sloane*, she'd say, shaking Andie's tiny hand. *We're happy to have you.*

Ding!

The elevator doors opened to reveal a marble lobby, the walls covered with photographs of models on catwalks all over the world, framed advertisements of models awash in stilettos and luxury handbags. A slender young woman with bulgy fish eyes breezed past, and Andie recognized her immediately as Shiraz Artillion, the new face of Chanel. She grabbed Lola's arm and took a deep breath. Hyperventilating in the Ford lobby didn't exactly say Top Model.

The silver Ford logo hung above a chrome reception desk that looked like something out of an episode of *Star Trek*. A woman with a Kool-Aid red pixie cut handed a folder to the male receptionist, who wore guyliner.

Lola strode across the room, Andie following close behind. "Hello, I'm Lola *Childs*," she announced, putting emphasis on her last name. "And this is Andie. We're meeting with Ayana Bennington." Lola tapped the toe of one of her Gap ballet flats against the marble floor.

The red-haired woman's whole body perked up. "We've been expecting you." She smiled. "Let me show you in." She held the door open and pointed to a giant gold office just inside the hall. A wall of windows overlooked Fifth Avenue. On the building across the way, a window washer was perched on scaffolding, drinking a Colt 45.

Andie looked at the desk. There, going through the latest edition of *Vogue* with a highlighter, was the mistress of her destiny. Her long hair was secured in a massive bun by three sets of black lacquered chopsticks. She stood when she saw them. "Ayana Bennington," she cooed. "It's fabulous to finally meet you."

"I'm Lola," Lola said, shaking Ayana's hand.

Andie smoothed back her hair. *Be fierce,* she thought, channeling her inner Tyra. *Be fierce.* She straightened up and looked Ayana directly in the eye—just like all the modeling blogs had told her to do when first meeting an agent. "I'm Andie," she said confidently, making sure to enunciate every syllable. (*Diction is done with the tip of the tongue and the teeth!*) Then she pulled her shoulders back and lifted her neck—*elongate!*—before sticking out her hand.

Ayana gestured to the two massive leather chairs in front of her desk. Andie sat down in one, her feet barely touching the floor. Lola sat beside her.

Ayana clasped her hands together and leaned forward, her gaze shifting to Lola. "I saw you at Fashion Week. I should have known you were Emma's daughter—I'd recognize those beautiful green eyes anywhere."

Lola adjusted her headband, her face a deep red.

"I was there too!" Andie offered. "I loved Alexander's fall collection," she added, ready to gush about the metallics and clean lines.

"Yes, that's right." Ayana nodded. "I remember you now." She eyed Andie carefully, and Andie kept her chin high and her neck long. "You must look more like your father."

"Actually, Andie's my stepsister," Lola corrected. "Or, well, she will be, really soon," she said quickly, shooting Andie a smile. "Our parents are getting married tomorrow!"

Andie tried to smile back, but her face was stiff, like her nana's after a round of Botox injections. No, she didn't have bright green eyes and blond hair, but was it *so* ridiculous to think she could be related to Emma Childs?

"Well, Lola . . ." Ayana scanned Lola's body. "You're stunning. Exquisite bone structure."

Andie dug her fingernails into the black leather chair. What? *Lola* was stunning? *Lola* was exquisite? Andie pinched Lola's arm, waiting for her to tell Ayana why they were really there.

Lola focused on a potted plant next to Ayana's desk, a little embarrassed. *Stunning, exquisite, stunning.* No one had ever said those words before—at least not when talking about *her. Dorky, clumsy, bowlegged*. Those were words you used to describe Lola Childs.

"I'm sure you hear that all the time." Ayana folded her thin arms over her chest.

Lola sat frozen, the compliments swirling around her head like snow in a snow globe. This whole week she'd felt like a circus freak in a Bloomingdale's catalog. She'd half expected Cate and Stella to put her in a cage and charge admission to see her. It felt good to hear Ayana Bennington—agent extraordinaire—compliment her.

When Lola lifted her head, Ayana was staring at her, waiting for a response. "Right," she said in a small voice, the tiniest smile creeping over her face. "All the time."

Andie clenched her hands into fists and let out a deep breath. This was supposed to be *her* moment, *her* big break. This is what *she* had been studying and practicing and hoping for. She kicked Lola under the desk, trying to get her attention, but Lola just rubbed her leg.

"How old did you say you were?" Ayana pressed. She took one of the chopsticks out of her hair, which stayed miraculously in place, and tapped it lightly against the glossy desktop.

"I'm interested in modeling too," Andie blurted out.

Ayana scanned Andie's tiny frame and pressed her lips together. She put her fingers to her temples, as if Andie had just spoken Portuguese and her brain was slowly trying to translate it. "Well," she began, "you have a beautiful complexion. Delicate features. There's a real warmth to your look, especially your eyes."

Andie straightened up in her chair and blushed happily. Ayana was talking about *her*. Forget Shiraz Artillion—*she'd* be the new face of Chanel, clutching a bottle of Coco perfume against her cheek, her hair slicked back.

Ayana rested her chin in her hands. "You have a more . . . *commercial* look. When Emma comes in we should discuss catalog work. We could start with JCPenney, Sears, Kohl's."

Andie felt her eyes welling with tears. Catalog work? In the modeling world, Ayana might as well have told her she should do dog food commercials. She wanted to go to bed, curl up under her red duvet, and not come out until she was five-foot seven . . . if she ever *was* five-foot seven. She was starting to feel like she belonged on *Little People, Big World.*

Ayana placed a hand on her computer mouse and pulled up her calendar on the screen. "I'd love for you to come in for some test shots," she said, peering over the desk at Lola—gangly giantess Lola, with ears that Andie could've used for extra shoe storage.

Lola clapped her hands together excitedly. "That would be brilliant!" she cried. She'd never thought about modeling before, but actually, it really *would* be brilliant. She and Andie could *both* be models. Every Ashton seventh-grader would worship her, whether she wore days-of-the-week knickers or not. Cate and Stella would seethe with jealousy over her billboard in Times Square. And if Kyle didn't fancy her now, he definitely would then. Forget the rehearsal dinner—she'd bring him to every Ashton Prep formal for the next six years. As her *boyfriend.*

Andie sank lower in her chair. She wished she could disappear, that she could suddenly just be somewhere else—a *Star Wars* convention, a medieval torture chamber—anywhere but here.

This was all Lola's fault. *She* was the one who'd e-mailed Ford. *She* was the one who'd let Ayana ramble on and on about how *stunning* she was. And now she was agreeing to do test shots!

Andie saw herself posing next to a jungle gym in OshKosh overalls, her hair in pigtails, while Lola graced the cover of *Teen Vogue, CosmoGirl!,* and *Seventeen.* She saw the Chanel ad again, but this time it was *Lola* clutching the bottle of perfume—*her* hair slicked back, exposing her massive ears.

Andie closed her eyes and let out a sigh. After everything, she'd been right: Modeling *was* her destiny. Modeling for *Sears.*

CARE FOR SOME TEA WITH THAT HUMBLE PIE?

Priya pulled a cucumber sandwich off the three-tier silver serving tray and leaned over to Sophie. "I cannot wait to see that silk dress in *Vogue*. I'm going to be like—*I* wore that!" She took a tiny bite out of the fluffy white bread.

"I know!" Sophie squealed. "I can't wait to see that tweed skirt I tried on."

Stella stirred a teaspoon of sugar into her china cup and gazed up at the marshmallow clouds on the domed ceiling of the rotunda. The entire cab ride to the Pierre, Blythe, Sophia, and Priya had kept on about Marc Jacobs' new collection. Sophie had been so distracted, she'd almost left the dress Cate bought her in the cab. Stella glanced across the table at Cate, who was stabbing at her scone with her fork dejectedly. Stella took a sip of her raspberry tea.

It had never tasted so sweet.

"Should we vote now?" Stella cooed, looking around the table at the girls.

"Yeah, let's do it." Sophie pulled a small black Moleskine notebook out of her quilted purse.

Blythe was smoothing some crème fraîche onto her scone but suddenly dropped her knife, her eyes fixed on something across the room. "Oh. My. God." she squeaked.

All the girls turned. At the table by the far wall, a man with a mop of blond hair was sitting with a woman who looked like a young, pre-surgery Demi Moore. He wore a tight black sports coat and had cheekbones more defined than Webster's dictionary. Cate straightened up in her chair. "Is that . . . *Harley Cross*?" she asked, smoothing down her dark brown hair. A young waiter with a shiny black ponytail set down Harley's check, her face a bright pink.

"It *is*," Priya cried, leaning her chin on her hand.

Sophie pinched her cheeks and pressed her lips together. "Wait—how do I look?" she asked. "Guys?" But no one took their eyes off Harley. He pushed his chair back and stood up, grabbing the woman's hand. The two of them headed toward the door as the table of overdressed Long Island girls next to them exploded in chatter.

"He's leaving?" Cate whined. She had been obsessed with Harley Cross since fifth grade, when she'd seen him in *Reinventing Simon Worth*, a romantic comedy about a first-grade teacher in England. Harley Cross was one of the most adorable actors in Hollywood *and* he had a British accent. British accents on funguslike stepsisters were annoying, but British accents on moppy-haired actors? Totally hot.

Harley glanced around the circular room, his eyes landing on

Cate. He held up one finger to the woman with him, then turned and started walking straight toward their table. Cate pulled at the silver locket on her neck, her pulse quickening. Harley ran a hand through his blond hair and tucked one finger in the front pocket of his dark-wash jeans.

Cate took her napkin off her lap, preparing to stand up and say hello, but as he got closer Cate realized he wasn't looking at her. He was staring at Stella, who was sitting in the chair beside her. He leaned down and gave her a kiss on the cheek.

"Hello, luv," he cooed. "I thought that was you. I'm flying back to London in three hours, but I couldn't walk out of here without saying hello."

"Hi." Stella grinned, her cheeks a rosy pink.

"So how's mum?" Harley asked. Cate coughed, trying to draw attention to herself, but Harley was still staring at Stella intently. Cate could feel the chewed-up scone sitting in her stomach like cement.

"Quite well," Stella replied.

Harley pulled back the bottom of his sport coat and rested a hand on his hip. "And your father . . . how is he keeping on?" he asked slowly, furrowing his brow in concern.

Stella looked down at the pink paisley carpeting, her eyes blurring from all the ornate swirls. "Um . . . fine," she said after a beat, then let out an uncomfortable laugh.

"Right. Well, it was good seeing you, Stella. Do send everyone my love." Harley squeezed Stella's shoulder, then walked off.

The second he disappeared from the rotunda, Sophie started shrieking. "Omigodomigodomigod!" she cried. Blythe tucked a piece of dirty blond hair behind her ear and wiped her forehead, still glowing from her Close Encounter of the Celebrity Kind.

Cate glanced around the table at the Chi Beta Phis, who were all staring at Stella like she'd done a magic trick. She twisted her cloth napkin in her hands. *For my next trick,* she imagined Stella saying, *I will make all your friends disappear.*

"That was amazing." Priya turned her chair toward Stella. "How do you know Harley Cross?" A woman in an unflattering mauve frock sat down near the entrance to the rotunda and began to play a gold harp, moving her graying head in slow figure eights.

"We're old family friends." Stella shrugged, as if to say, *There are more celebrities where that came from.* She smoothed down the front of her tan skirt, then looked around the table. Priya, Sophie, and Blythe were seriously impressed. This was better than bringing the basketball team to Jackson Hole, better than getting them into the Marc Jacobs designer showroom. She *knew* Harley Cross. And this was what they'd think about when they scribbled her name across their ballots. "Should we vote now?" Stella prompted again, smiling sweetly at Cate.

Cate balled up her white napkin in her hand and threw it down on the table. She couldn't let this vote slip away from her. She was the head of the Chi Beta Phis—she always had been, and she always would be.

Cate cleared her throat. "First we should voice any concerns we have about potential candidates," Cate said carefully, leveling her eyes at Stella. "Sure, Harley Cross knows Stella, but how much do *we* really know about her?" At the table next to them, a balding waiter leaned over and poured a scalding cup of tea, nearly searing off his eyebrows. Cate breathed in the minty smell, her whole body tingling with excitement.

"What do you mean?" Blythe asked, confused.

"Stella's father cheated on her mother with Cloud McClean— the same Cloud McClean that sings 'Kick It' and wears metallic unitards. She didn't leave London because it was 'so over,' and her parents aren't 'best mates.'" Cate made quotes with her fingers to remind everyone of Stella's exact words. "She lied about that, and I'm sure she's lied about plenty of other things," Cate finished. Across the table, Stella stared into her lap.

"Is that true?" Priya asked.

"So your father didn't get a job in Australia?" Sophie asked.

"No," Cate answered the question for her. "He didn't."

"And you said my dad 'had issues'?" Blythe asked, digging her fingernail into the egg sandwich on her plate. "That was so . . ."

"Mean," Cate cut in.

"Not cool," Priya continued. "Why didn't you just tell us?"

"I—" Stella began.

"If you'd just told us, nobody would have cared. But you've been lying to us since we first met you." Priya crossed her arms over her chest.

"My point exactly," Cate said coolly. "Chi Beta Phis don't keep secrets from one another." She appraised her stepsister. Stella's chin was quivering, and she still hadn't looked up. Whatever—it was time to vote, and Cate couldn't get all remorseful now. She grabbed Sophie's notebook and yanked out five pieces of paper, handing one out to each girl.

Finally Stella lifted her head. "Wait a second. I think it's my turn to *voice concerns*," she said icily, staring up at Cate's purplish blue eyes. She'd make sure Cate regretted mentioning anything about her mum and dad. "Because frankly, I'm concerned Cate isn't able to keep things . . . *confidential*." If Cate wanted to fight with secrets, Stella had a whole arsenal of them. "What's that you said about Blythe? That she's a spray tan addict? That she's never even been to Mexico?"

Blythe emitted a sound like a squeak toy.

"I—I didn't say that," Cate stammered, sitting back down at the table. Her whole body was shaking.

"Oh, yes, you did." Stella pressed on. "And then you kept on about how Sophie still plays with Barbies—how she keeps them under her bathroom sink."

Priya covered her mouth with her hand and giggled. "You do?"

"I'm a *collector*!" Sophie yelled, pushing up the sleeves of her blue silk dress defensively.

"I'm not addicted," Blythe said through gritted teeth. "And I was in Cabo just last spring."

Priya was still giggling with her hand over her mouth, looking back and forth between her friends.

"And Priya doesn't go to sleepaway camp in the Adirondacks," Stella continued. "She goes to science camp. Isn't she *obsessed* with dissecting things?"

Priya fell silent.

Stella leaned back in her chair and smiled. She had just dropped a gossip bomb on Cate's perfect little world, blowing it to pieces.

Cate pressed her palms down on the table, leaning toward the girls. "I didn't say that—I swear," she lied.

"You were the only one I told!" Priya cried.

Cate just shrugged, looking at the girls like she was just as surprised as they were. For now, she would use the strategy she always used when she was caught in a lie: deny, deny, deny.

"Forget it, Priya," Blythe growled. "Let's vote." She pulled a pen from the pile on the table and eyed Stella and Cate. Then she scribbled something on her makeshift ballot and folded it up.

"Yeah," Sophie agreed, grabbing two pens and passing one to Priya. As the girls scribbled on their ballots, Cate was suddenly nervous. That hadn't gone *quite* the way she had planned. Yes, she had said those things about the girls, but they had all known she was never good at keeping secrets. In seventh grade she'd accidentally told her entire health class that Blythe shaved her toes. They wouldn't hold it against her, would they? She picked up a pen and wrote her name slowly in perfect script, crossing the *t* so hard she nearly ripped through the paper.

Blythe collected the votes from each girl, read them silently, and placed them facedown on the table so nobody could see. She looked at Stella, then at Cate, her face as expressionless as a world champion poker player's.

Cate smoothed down the hem of her dress and held her breath.

"Stella . . ." Blythe said slowly, looking across the table. Priya held her hands in a tight ball in front of her mouth. "You did *not* win the vote." Stella's face fell, and she stared glumly at the serving dish of scones.

Cate exhaled and her arms sprang up in excitement. She was sorry for ever doubting her friends, for thinking they would vote for some British newbie over her. They were behind her, *always*, no matter what. Cate rested her hands on the table and stood up slowly, looking at Priya, Blythe, and Sophie. "Thank you," she said. "And I'm so, so sorry for telling Stella all your secrets."

"I'm a *collector*," Sophie whispered again, to no one in particular.

"And I promise you," Cate said, grabbing Blythe's orange arm, "this is going to be our best year at Ashton yet. You guys are the best friends anyone could ask for."

Blythe smirked. "Thanks for the touching speech. But actually, Cate, you didn't win either—*I did*."

Cate stared down at Blythe—the same Blythe who'd practically lived at her house last summer. The same Blythe who had insisted her mother escort both Cate *and* Blythe to Ashton Prep's mother-daughter tea. Cate grabbed the stack of votes from Blythe's lap and shuffled through them. Sophie had written Blythe's name in bubble letters, the same way she doodled on her notebooks. Cate recognized Priya's handwriting, then Blythe's. There were two other sheets of paper: one that said *Stella*, and one in her own handwriting that said *Cate*, a tiny crown drawn over the C. She crumpled the votes up in her hand.

"You were right . . ." Blythe continued. "I am tired of being so 'behind the scenes' . . . 'in your shadow.'" Cate cringed when she heard her own words fired back at her. Blythe took a bite of a chocolate éclair and closed her eyes. "Mmmm . . . delish," she hummed. Cate thought back to when she'd cornered Blythe in the Jackson Hole bathroom like some small, frightened animal. While she and Stella were battling it out at Marc Jacobs, stupidly caught up in their sister war, Blythe had swept in and stolen the Chi Beta Phis out from under her.

Blythe glanced at Priya and Sophie. "Well, we should get going." She stood up and dropped her napkin on the table, then leveled her eyes at Cate. "You'll get the check, right? I have a fake tan habit to support."

"Yeah," Priya said, "and I have to go hack up some squirrels."

Blythe strode out of the rotunda, Priya and Sophie on either side of her. They were swinging their slick black Marc Jacobs shopping bags—with the dresses and shoes *Cate* had bought for them.

Cate stood there frozen, wondering if this was the last time she'd ever have lunch with her friends. After all, they weren't really *her* friends anymore—they were *Blythe's*.

SORRY, UGLY DUCKLING, SOME THINGS NEVER CHANGE

Lola followed Andie down Eighty-second Street, practically running to keep up with her. They'd walked the almost two miles home, and Andie hadn't said a word to her. Lola had apologized, but the truth was, she didn't feel *that* sorry. How was she supposed to know catalog work was for *America's Next Top Model* rejects? She had never seen the show!

Lola adjusted her headband and walked confidently toward the town house. She couldn't stop thinking about her meeting with Ayana Bennington. A chorus of *stunning! exquisite! stunning!* echoed in her head.

On the sidewalk ahead of her, a woman who shouldn't have been wearing spandex was kneeling down, letting her cocker spaniel practically French-kiss her. Lola looked at her Hello Kitty watch. It was five fifty-five. Which meant Kyle would arrive any minute. They were going to hang out in Central Park before the rehearsal dinner, and she would ask him to be her plus-one. Sure it was short notice, but boys didn't need that long to get ready.

Not ones as cute as Kyle, anyway. He could wear ripped-up jeans and a white Hanes T-shirt and still look perfect.

She smoothed down Stella's Juicy cropped jacket and imagined her and Kyle at the dinner, sitting next to each other at some restaurant called Capitale. They'd spend the whole time making fun of the wide-brimmed hat her grandmother insisted on wearing indoors, or shaking salt and pepper in Stella's drink whenever she turned around.

Andie threw open the wrought iron gate and stomped inside. Lola followed her into the foyer, the heavy black door nearly slamming her in the nose. There, right next to the staircase, was Kyle. "Hi!" she cried.

"Sorry to surprise you—your mom let me in." Kyle looked around the expansive oak-paneled foyer, his warm brown eyes finally landing on Lola.

Andie stepped in front of Lola and stuck out her tiny hand. "Hi . . ." she cooed, tossing her shiny brown hair over her shoulder the way she'd showed Lola. "I'm Andie."

Lola fiddled with the buttons on her jacket, suddenly nervous. She'd nearly forgotten Andie was there.

"Hey." Kyle smiled, his face turning pink. He looked back to Lola. "Did you still want to go to the park?"

But before Lola could respond, Andie touched her Kate Spade wedge to Kyle's blue-and-white Adidas Gazelles, recognizing the indoor soccer shoes. "You play?" she asked.

"Yeah, I'm on the team at Donalty." Kyle nodded.

"I play at Ashton." Andie tugged at the highlight in her bangs, trying to ignore Lola's glare. Sure, flirting with Kyle was wrong, but Lola deserved it. She'd stolen her chance at Ford. Maybe she didn't agree with everything Chi Beta Phi did, but after observing them for years, she'd learned the art of revenge. "A bunch of us scrimmage in Central Park on Tuesdays with some of the guys from Haverford," she said casually, knowing that all the boys from Donalty worshipped Haverford's nationally ranked team.

"Sweet." Kyle nodded. "Can anyone come? I'm actually—" he began, but Lola cut him off.

"We should get going," Lola said shrilly, moving toward the door.

But Kyle didn't budge. "So are you excited for the wedding?" he asked Andie. "I think my parents are making me wear a tux tomorrow." He pointed a finger gun across his chest. "James Bond style."

Lola adjusted her headband. This was her chance. *Just say it,* she thought. "*I'm* very excited!" she cried, a little too loudly. "My mum said we could all bring someone to the rehearsal dinner tonight." She looked into Kyle's chocolate brown eyes, waiting for him to realize that that "someone" was him.

"Yeah," Andie added, stepping so close to Kyle they could've been Siamese twins. "Would you want to be my date?" She twirled a strand of hair around her finger.

Kyle glanced at Lola, as though he needed her permission. She wanted to say something but her mouth felt dry, like she'd just eaten a whole box of chalk. *No,* she thought, *don't!*

"That sounds awesome," Kyle finally said, smoothing his Zac Efron bangs off his forehead with a smile.

Lola felt the tears welling up in her eyes. Kyle was going to the rehearsal dinner with Andie? It was like peanut butter with pickles: just *wrong*. She bit her lip. She wasn't going to let Kyle see her cry.

She grabbed the front door and pulled it open. "Well, you better get ready then!" she snapped, motioning at the open door. "The dinner is at eight."

"Um . . . what about the park? We still have time for a walk," Kyle stammered, glancing at his watch. He inched toward the door nervously, waiting for Lola.

But instead of joining him, Lola pushed the door closed, nearly crushing him.

"See you tonight, Kyle!" Andie cried sweetly, waving.

Lola locked the door, with Kyle on the other side.

She turned to Andie and gritted her teeth. *See you never, is more like it.* "You know I fancy Kyle," she hissed, wiping her face with the back of her hand. She wanted to grab the blue porcelain vase off the credenza and chuck it at Andie's head. Just when Kyle had started to like *her*—to think *she* was pretty—Andie had waltzed in and ruined everything.

"Well, *you* know how much I wanted to be a model!" Andie screamed, her face turning a purplish red. "I can't believe you told Ayana Bennington you'd come in for test shots!"

"Sorry if not everyone in the universe thinks I'm ugly!" Lola yelled back, hot tears streaming down her face.

"What's going on here?" Winston emerged from the kitchen, his suit jacket slung over his shoulder. "You girls are supposed to be getting ready for the rehearsal dinner."

Emma followed close behind, in a gray silk dress and black patent leather heels. Her wavy blond hair was pulled back into a messy I-don't-want-this-to-look-like-it-took-an-hour-but-it-did bun. "Lola," Emma said, looking at her daughter's tearstained face. "What happened?"

Lola ran toward Emma, burying her face in the front of her silk dress. "I hate her!" she cried.

Just then the front door swung open.

"Well, maybe if you hadn't blabbed everything I said about them, things would have been different!" Cate yelled. She stormed up the stairs.

"Me?" Stella cried, following her into the house and slamming the door. "I was your bloody slave all week! You had me running around like some nitwit, organizing your closet!"

"Why on earth are you two yelling?" Winston asked, scratching the back of his neck so hard he left white marks.

Cate froze on the top step, Stella just below, as they realized they had an audience.

Stella squeezed the banister, annoyed. She didn't have time to explain to Winston how Cate had told all her mates about the scandal with Cloud McClean. The rag mags would probably be calling the house any minute, offering him money for an exclusive interview (*Emma's Fiancé Speaks!*).

"You just couldn't stand that your mates liked me better than you—could you?" Stella hissed.

"*You* don't know anything about *my* friends!" Cate clutched the silver locket around her neck and her eyes welled with tears. Stella had been in New York for a millisecond. Cate was the one who'd sat on the bench at swimming lessons and claimed leg cramps the first time Blythe got her period. Cate was the one who'd been there the first time Priya put on makeup, and Cate was the one who'd taught Sophie how to shave her legs when her mom said she was too young. "Did you even have any friends in London? Or did you just run around stealing everyone else's?"

"Mum." Stella turned to Emma. "I'm not going to the bleeding rehearsal dinner—not with *her*."

Cate crossed her arms over her chest and glared at Winston. "Don't worry about it! I'm not going either!" she spat, storming up the stairs to her bedroom.

"Cate Sloane!" Winston called up the staircase. But she was already gone.

Emma put her fingers to her temples and winced like she had eaten ice cream too quickly and was having a brain freeze.

"She's bloody awful," Stella muttered through clenched teeth. Then her gaze fell on Lola, who was still standing at Emma's side. "You nicked my shirts!" she cried, recognizing her cropped Juicy jacket. "Those better be back in my room in ten minutes or you're dead." She pointed her finger at Lola and then turned and trudged up the stairs.

Winston and Emma stood stock-still, as though someone had just driven a truck through the foyer and smashed everything to pieces. Winston looked at Andie, his skin splotchy, the way it always was when he was stressed. "What happened?" he asked again, glancing from her to Lola.

An hour later, Cate sat on the leather couch in the den next to Lola, Stella, and Andie. She peeled off her petal pink manicure, trying to pretend she was anywhere but here.

She'd sat in her room for half an hour frantically texting Priya, Sophie, and Blythe. She'd tried apologizing (IM SO SO SORRY, U HAVE NO IDEA HOW SORRY I M), flattery (U HAVE THE BEST TAN AT ASHTON, SRSLY), and even bribery (SHOPPING ON MONDAY? ON ME?) but none of them had responded. She'd tried to distract herself by organizing her shoe closet, half expecting her dad to knock on her door and force her to go to the rehearsal dinner. But he hadn't. Instead he and Emma had called a "family meeting," asking the girls to come into the den "to talk."

Winston and Emma stood in front of the leather couch, their hands fused together. Cate glanced at her Tiffany watch. It was seven thirty, and the rehearsal dinner was supposed to start at eight. But Emma had changed out of her gray silk gown and into blue terry-cloth pajamas that even Cate's nana wouldn't have worn. Her eyes looked puffy and red, like she was having an allergy attack. Cate hoped that was the case. Her stomach tightened.

"We need to talk about what's been going on with you girls," Winston said sternly. His eyes scanned the couch.

Emma wrung her hands and looked at her oldest daughter. "Stella," she began, "what were you two keeping on about? I've never seen you act like that before."

Stella glanced sideways at Cate. Cate had followed her home from the Pierre, reciting point by point why she was right and Stella was wrong. If Stella had to hear—one more time—how she was a fungus on Cate's life, she was getting on the next plane back to London. She would call the cab herself. "Nothing," Stella lied. "Just forget it."

"I will not forget it," her mom said, raising her voice. She pinched her earlobe, at the pressure point her acupuncturist had told her would relieve headaches. "Cate?" Emma pressed. "Can you tell me what's going on?"

Cate peeled the polish off her pinkie nail and flicked it on the floor. "I really don't want to talk about it," she said flatly, staring at the sapphire ring on her finger. Emma could sleep in the master bedroom, but she'd never be her mother—Cate didn't have to answer any of her questions. "We'll go to the rehearsal dinner, if that's what you want."

"That is not the point!" Winston snapped. "Tomorrow at four o'clock Emma and I are supposed to get married. And you girls can't even look at one another." He let out a deep breath. Then he turned to Andie and Lola. "Do you girls have anything to say for yourselves?"

Andie bit her lip and stared at her dad. After a few hours of solitary confinement, she did feel a little badly about the whole Kyle thing. But every time she thought about Lola modeling for Ford, standing on a beach, her hair blown back by a giant fan, a knot formed in her throat, like she'd swallowed a softball. Lola had agreed to test shots. And then she'd cried to Emma, saying she *hated* Andie.

"Why don't you ask Lola about her meeting with Ayana Bennington?" Andie said crisply, crossing her arms over her chest. She couldn't wait to see how Emma would react when she found out precious, innocent Lola had been dropping her name all over Manhattan.

"Lola!" Emma cried sharply. "What is *that* about?"

"I did that for you!" Lola growled at Andie, pressing her fists into the tops of her thin legs.

"That is quite enough!" Emma cried. "Quite enough." She slapped her hand on the coffee table.

Winston wrapped his arm around her. "We can't get married like this—we won't," he said sadly, looking across the couch at the girls. He shook his head as though four strangers had walked into his house, masquerading as Lola, Cate, Andie, and Stella. "The wedding's off."

RECLAIMING THE CASTLE

Andie's stomach let out a loud, wild-animal growl. She wrapped her arms around her sides and walked down the hallway, toward the mahogany staircase. She could add "missed dinner" to her list of HOW THIS DAY WENT HORRIBLY WRONG, right under "rejected by Ayana Bennington," "betrayed by stepsister," and "helped ruin father's wedding."

She stopped at the top of the stairs and stood listening to her father's muffled voice in the study. She tiptoed toward the door and pushed it open a crack. Winston was pacing back and forth across the room, clutching the cordless phone.

"No, it's the kids," he said, holding the back of his neck in his hand. "We've decided to postpone the wedding . . . indefinitely." Winston paused. "Yes, I understand. Thanks, Gloria." He set the phone down on the rolltop desk. It was dark outside and he was still in his suit for the rehearsal dinner, except now his crisp blue shirt was unbuttoned, and he was walking around in his black dress socks. He caught a glimpse of Andie's reflection in the window and turned around, his face drawn, his eyes red and wet.

Andie grabbed the bottom of her T-shirt, suddenly nervous. "Daddy?" she asked, her voice trembling. Winston coughed and rubbed his face with both hands. She hadn't seen her father cry since her mom died.

"Yes?" Winston muttered, not looking Andie in the eye. Before he could say anything else, Andie ran toward him and wrapped her arms around him in a tight hug. She rested her cheek against his chest and tried to swallow the lump in her throat. She couldn't stand seeing her father sad. She wished she could rewind the whole night—the whole week, even—and just start over.

"Dad, I—" She sniffed back her tears. "I'm so sorry. I didn't mean to ruin the wedding."

Winston rubbed Andie's back. "You didn't ruin anything," he said, shaking his head. "I'm the one who should be sorry. I was just—" His voice sounded like it might crack. He coughed loudly and rested his hands on Andie's shoulders. "I was just so excited about Emma, and you girls seemed like you were getting along so well. I got carried away and rushed everything. I never should have pushed you girls—you weren't ready for this." He kissed Andie twice on the top of her head.

"I was fine, Dad, really," Andie whispered.

"We've all had a long day," he said, starting for the door. "Let's talk more about this tomorrow." And with that, he rubbed Andie's cheek and walked out of the study.

• • •

Andie sat at the cherrywood table and stared down at the snack she'd made for herself—blue cheese with baby carrots and celery. The food suddenly looked unappetizing, like seagull-poop crudités. She walked over to the garbage and emptied the plate into the bin.

In the recycling box, sitting on top of a stack of salmon pink *Financial Times*es, was an unopened card addressed to Emma and Winston. Andie picked up the beige envelope and held it in her hands. As she ripped it open, a photo of Winston and Emma tumbled out. Winston had his hand on Emma's back and was leaning in close to her, smiling, as though he were telling her the most amazing secret.

It was from their uncle Paul, who had just broken his leg in a motorcycle accident on the Pacific Coast Highway. *Dear Winston and Emma,* it read. *If only I had used my turn signal, I could be telling you this in person! Congratulations on the wedding. Emma—thank you for making my brother so incredibly happy.*

Andie set the card down on the counter, unable to read another word. Her stomach lurched as she imagined sitting in the den tomorrow, sprawled out on the couch watching *The Hills*, when her dad and Emma should have been getting married.

Just then Lola walked into the kitchen in her Harry Potter pajamas. When she saw Andie she yanked open the refrigerator door.

Andie could hear the plastic drawers opening and closing. "Lola—look at this," Andie said slowly, holding out the wedding card to the back of the fridge door.

Lola slammed it shut. "I can't believe you're trying to talk to me!" she said, her eyes welling with tears. "You practically snogged Kyle right there in the foyer." She still had her headband on, but her hair was pulled back in a ponytail and her eyes were swollen. "I really fancied him," she said again, her voice cracking.

Andie turned the card over in her hands, not wanting to look Lola in the eye. She hadn't felt so guilty since she'd spit in Cate's Clinique eye cream, payback for Cate telling the entire sixth grade Andie was adopted. Sure Cate had deserved it, but Andie hadn't wanted her to get pinkeye or anything.

Andie tugged the blond highlight in her bangs. "I'm sorry," she muttered. "But I really don't like Kyle—I swear."

Lola hugged a jar of gherkins to her chest. "You don't?" she asked.

"No!" Andie cried. "I barely know him! I was just mad about what happened at Ford."

"That agent only liked me because of my mum!" Lola said, her nose twitching. "She's already sent me two e-mails asking for Mum's mobile number. Look at me—I'm not a bloody model." Lola pointed at her bare toes, which pointed inward like they were kissing each other. "I'm bowlegged! And my ears stick out like Dumbo." She lifted up one side of her headband so Andie could see.

Andie looked at Lola's big ears and couldn't help but laugh. "No, Lola, I think Ayana really did like you. You should do the test shots. What do you have to lose?" Andie shrugged, deciding then and there that she was over the Ford snub. Yeah, Ayana Bennington was a famous agent, but she wasn't the only one out there. Andie had already gone to the yellow pages online and found three listings—all looking for tween models. After all, your first agency rejection was a rite of passage. Tyra, Kate, even Twiggy all had to face adversity before they got their big breaks.

Andie grabbed the picture of Winston and Emma. "My dad was calling Gloria in the study and he was . . ." Her voice trembled. "Really upset—really, *really* upset."

"My mum was crying before, in the den." Lola took the picture from Andie's hand and studied it. Then she pressed her hands into her cheeks. "We can fix things," she suddenly cried. "We have to!"

"Yeah . . ." Andie agreed. "But how?" It was over. The damage was done.

Lola clapped her hands. "*They* want to get married. We just need to prove *we* want them to." Her green eyes were wide. "I have an idea."

THE ICE QUEEN MELTS

Stella opened the pantry and moved a jar of kalamata olives, looking for some pita bread. After unpacking the last of her beauty supplies and "Dress Tops III," reclaimed from Lola's room, she'd crept out of her room to scavenge for food. She found Andie and Lola in the kitchen, sitting at the round table in the atrium, whispering secretively, as though they were plotting to nick a Van Gogh from the Met.

"That's brilliant, Andie!" Lola cried, scribbling something down on a pad of paper.

Stella looked at them curiously. They had gone from wanting to kill each other to being best mates in less than four hours. She, however, intended to never speak to Cate again.

And if their parents really were splitting up, maybe she wouldn't have to.

Stella pulled a pita from the plastic wrap and took a bite, the flour dusting her lips. Even if Cate *had* been a nitwit, Stella kept thinking about her mum's swollen eyes. When her mum had walked into the den earlier, Stella's head had spun—she'd felt like she was back in her kitchen in London last year, the day her mum and dad had told her about the divorce. Stella had just stared at the grandfather clock against the wall, tears welling in her eyes. But everything had changed when her mum met Winston—she'd stopped disappearing into her room whenever "Kick It" came on the radio; she'd stopped spending hours sitting at the dining room table, looking through old family photos from holidays in Nice and Morocco.

Lola sat back in her chair and squealed. "We can buy streamers and pick flowers from Central Park!"

Stella took another bite of her pita and walked toward the foyer, curious.

"We could probably get the Ashton band to play," Andie said. "And maybe you could play Pachelbel's Canon on your viola."

Stella stopped in the doorway. It sounded like Andie and Lola were planning a party. A really, really lame party. Stella hadn't seen a streamer since Lola's ninth birthday, and even then they weren't cool. "What are you doing?" she asked, narrowing her eyes at the girls.

"Um . . ." Andie muttered. "We just—we want to do something for my dad and your mom. We were thinking of having a wedding for them . . . in the garden?" She waited for Stella to laugh, but Stella just tilted her head to the side, thinking.

"Hmph." Stella *did* want to do something for her mum, but a garden wedding seemed like a sad consolation prize—especially one planned by two clueless twelve-year-olds. They'd have the guests playing Twister and eating pizza and Twizzlers. Stella looked out the glass wall at the wide brick patio, which was lit up by one small lamp. She eyed the latticework archway in the corner, which had been practically devoured by ivy. A garden wedding would be hard to plan in one day, but the space had potential.

Lola pressed her hands to her cheeks. "We're going to make a cake!"

Stella shook her head and sat down next to them at the round cherry table. "No—definitely not. We should call Greene Street Bakery and get something simple, elegant, and ready-made. Mum loved the buttercream frosting." Stella stood and paced in front of the table. "And then we have to find a caterer and a photographer." Lola diligently scribbled each of Stella's instructions on the pad. "We'll need the numbers of everyone on the guest list, though. . . ." Stella trailed off.

Lola stopped writing and looked up, staring at something behind Stella. Stella turned to see Cate leaning against the door frame in her ballet-slipper pink J. Crew nightgown, her arms crossed over her chest. She'd clearly overheard everything. The last thing Stella needed was Cate telling her how daft she was for encouraging Andie and Lola to plan an impromptu wedding. Nowhere—not even the kitchen, at ten at night—was safe from Cate Sloane.

Cate ran her tongue over her teeth and walked into the atrium, snatching a raspberry folder off the granite island on her way. She pushed past Stella and sat down at the table next to Andie.

"If we're going to plan a wedding—this is our bible," Cate said, dropping it on the table. "Gloria gave it to Dad and Emma.

It has the guest list, the numbers for the photographer and the florist—everything."

Lola slowly nodded at Cate, like she wasn't sure if it was actually Cate talking or some nicer Cate imposter. "We should definitely get flowers from Anne Bruno—they're around the corner, and they could probably do some quick, simple center-pieces."

"It should just be family and close friends," Stella continued, tugging on her golden blond curls. "We could call them tomorrow morning. And Andie wanted to use the Ashton band." Stella winced.

"No way!" Cate let out a little laugh and poked Andie in the arm. "No one wants to dance to a flute solo of 'Hey Ya.'"

"That's what I thought too," Stella said, looking at Cate. For the first time all day, she didn't cringe when she looked into Cate's deep blue eyes.

"Well, now that we have the band's number, I can just tell them to come here, instead of the boathouse," Andie offered.

"We're going to plan a wedding!" Lola suddenly cried.

THE BELLES OF THE BALL

A flock of tuxedoed waiters slowly placed trays on the long buffet table. On the garden terrace above, the band was rehearsing. The lead singer's silver dress reflected the afternoon sun as though she were a human disco ball.

"In my life," she sang softly into the microphone, "I've loved you more." A balding man in a blue suit played a few chords on an electric keyboard, his head well on its way to sunburn.

"Throw me that tablecloth?" Cate asked, glancing at Stella. She set two crystal vases filled with exotic orchids down on the table. Stella picked up the pale green linen and tossed it to Cate, who nodded silently in thanks.

Cate wasn't over the whole Pierre incident, especially since she still hadn't heard from her friends. Not a text, not an IM—nothing. They must have talked to Gloria by now—she had called every person on the guest list, one by one, and told them the wedding had been postponed. If she didn't hear from Blythe by tonight, she would march over to her penthouse and demand answers . . . or, well, ask really nicely. For the first time ever, she wasn't in a place to demand anything.

Stella handed Cate a pile of folded napkins that reminded her of those silly newspaper hats kids made in elementary school. Cate had to admit, even if she and Stella were mad at each other, they made a fierce team. This morning they had delegated their hearts out, sending Lola to Godiva for party favors and Andie out for flower arrangements. Stella had whittled down the list of guests to a few dozen and called them all personally to invite them over. Then Cate had asked her aunt Celeste, Winston's younger sister, to call in favors to all her contacts at *Food & Wine* magazine, where she was editor in chief. Celeste had found them a caterer, waitstaff, and bar staff in less than two hours, and Andie had gotten the Ashfords across the street to donate the portable furniture they used for the Harvard Club socials they threw in their drawing room. In less than a day they had pulled together a wedding. Forget Gloria Rubenstein—the Sloane-Childs sisters were the power party planners in New York.

Cate straightened the thin white china plates. In a few minutes the guests would start arriving, and her parents would be there in an hour. The girls had made breakfast for them that morning as an apology, and Lola had told them they should keep their massage and haircut appointments at Red Door Salon that afternoon—to unwind. She'd even arranged for Winston's driver, George, to come pick them up.

In the corner of the garden Andie stood on a step stool, forcing one last rose into the latticework arch.

They were almost ready. As Cate centered the vase on the

table, her iPhone chimed. She pulled it out of the pocket of her Juicy terry pants and stared at it. It was a text . . . from *Blythe*.

"You too?" Stella asked, holding her iPhone up.

BLYTHE: P AND S WANT U IN, BUT I'M STILL PO'D. PUCKER UP, LADIES. U HAVE SOME KISSING UP TO DO THIS YEAR.

Cate imagined herself buying all of Blythe's new C-cup bras, proofreading all her English essays, and touching up her back with Neutrogena sunless tanning foam. She imagined spending every afternoon at *Blythe's* penthouse, in *Blythe's* room, sitting on *Blythe's* couch. Of course Cate still wanted to be part of the Chi Beta Phis. Ashton Prep would be impossible without her friends—like going to war with nothing but a butter knife. But Cate had swallowed enough pride these last two days—any more and she'd need her stomach pumped.

Stella tugged on a blond curl. "This is textual harassment," she muttered, shaking her head.

Cate laughed, despite herself.

"Cate! Andie!" Lola poked her head out of the dining room door. She was wearing a black Gap dress and clutching an armful of programs that Andie had spent the night designing and printing out. "Your uncle Mark is already here! You have to get dressed!"

Cate took one last look at her cell phone and tucked it back into her pocket. Then she slowly pulled out her Stila lip gloss. If she was going to have to kiss up to Blythe all year, she could at least make sure her lips were hydrated.

Back in her room, Cate pulled on her canary yellow Nanette Lepore dress. The girls had agreed to scrap the bridesmaid dresses for any dress they wanted to wear, as long as it was tasteful and elegant (Cate and Stella held veto rights on Lola and Andie's outfits, of course).

Cate spun around once in the mirror, but she didn't get the clothing high she usually did when she wore the yellow dress. Stella had been right all along about Blythe—she *had* wanted Cate's throne.

Cate pushed a black patent leather headband over her forehead and smoothed down her dark brown hair. Telling all the girls about Cloud McClean had been a little harsh. Fine—it wasn't just harsh. It was kind of . . . *wrong* . . . like pouring your cappuccino on someone's new white linen Prada dress. She'd gotten caught up in the vote. She'd just wanted so badly to win, and she'd seen it slipping away. But still . . .

Cate opened the door. Even from the hallway, she could hear the sounds of the guests arriving. She made her way down the stairs and saw her aunt Celeste in the foyer, petting Andie's head like Andie was one of her Saint Bernards.

"Cate!" Celeste cried, spotting her niece. In her cerulean Zac Posen dress, fresh off her second round of microdermabrasion, Celeste looked twenty-five. She grabbed Cate's hand and pulled her into the kitchen, pointing at the garden through the atrium's huge windows. "You, my dear, are absolutely amazing. Your father is going to be thrilled." The garden was packed with guests, downing their last drinks before the ceremony began. Greta, who always attended Cate's plays when Winston couldn't, was standing by the buffet, taste-testing the baby lamb chops.

"I know, it's—" Cate stopped, feeling like someone had shoved an hors d'oeuvre down her throat. Outside, Stella was standing by the bar . . . wearing *Cate's* dress. Cate could have spotted the embroidered yellow fabric out of three hundred racks at Barneys. "I'll be right back," she muttered.

She walked toward the door, watching as Stella sidled up to the bar and ordered a drink. Cate's mind raced. Maybe Stella had known Cate was going to wear it. Maybe she had seen it in her closet and gone out and bought it herself. It was from last season, though—one of the few pieces Cate still wore.

Stella was so busy squeezing lime into her Diet Coke, she didn't even notice Cate next to her.

The bartender, a hipster with a handlebar moustache, shook a silver cocktail shaker like a maraca. "You guys look like twins," he said. Stella turned and looked Cate up and down, her face a little pale.

"Nice dress," Cate said. Then she looked Stella in the eyes, her lips curling into a smile.

"You too," Stella said softly. "Though I have to say"—Stella pressed one finger into Cate's arm—"you look a little pale. Think we have time for a quick spray tan?"

"If I have to be bossed around this year by a burnt sienna crayon," Cate laughed, "at least I'll be in good company."

"Do you think maybe . . ." Stella began but trailed off.

"What?"

"Maybe we're better off on our own?" She raised a blond eyebrow. "Chi Sigma?"

Slowly, Cate nodded. "That could work."

EVER AFTER

Andie stood next to Cate, Lola, and Stella, gripping the stem of her rose bouquet tightly. Emma and Winston were holding hands under the flowered archway, reciting the last of their wedding vows. Andie had been so excited when her dad and Emma stepped into the garden, slowly taking in the band on the terrace, the round tables covered in crisp pale green linens, the vases overflowing with orchids. Emma had started crying when she spotted her brother Simon, and Winston had declared it was better than the wedding Gloria had planned at the boathouse. Emma had even changed into her Vera Wang wedding dress for the ceremony, and Winston wore his tux.

"I now pronounce you husband and wife," Judge Haines said, clasping his hands together. "You may kiss the bride."

Winston grinned mischievously. He dipped Emma and gave her a dramatic kiss on the lips. Emma let out a laugh and smacked him playfully on his jacket lapel. The guests, who had gathered around the archway, clapped. Greta turned the dial on her disposable camera with great effort, while Tatiana Petrov, the supermodel, pressed blotting paper to her dewy face.

Andie heard a sniffling sound and turned to Cate, who was dabbing at her eyes with the tip of her finger. "Are you crying?" Andie whispered. She smiled, satisfied. Any ceremony that could make Cate cry was a complete success.

"Definitely not," Cate whispered back, turning away. Maybe she *was* crying, but she'd rather spend every Friday night playing with Sophie's Barbies than admit that she was moved by her father's wedding—the same wedding that a day ago she'd hoped would never happen. Emma and Winston were facing the crowd of guests, their hands raised as though they were doing a curtain call on Broadway. Cate turned the sapphire ring around on her finger. Emma would never be her mother, but she *really* loved Cate's dad. And for now, that seemed like enough.

The band started playing classical music as the guests dispersed, milling about the garden. A few of Winston's old friends from Yale sat down by the bar, their table exploding in laughter every now and then. Emma's mother was sipping a dirty martini and talking loudly to her son Simon and his wife, a curvy woman in a magenta Valentino dress.

Emma lifted the hem of her mermaid gown and pulled Winston over to the girls. "Luvvies," she cooed, kissing Lola and Stella on the cheek.

Winston smoothed back Andie's bangs and wrapped Cate in a hug. "Thank you for this." He stepped back to take in the girls.

Lola threw her long arms around Winston's neck and stumbled

into him. "Cheers, Winston!" she cried. Winston slowly hugged her back, a little surprised.

"Cheers, Lola," he said, a smile breaking across his face. Next Lola hugged Stella, who couldn't help but laugh. Lola was like an excited puppy, running around and smothering everyone in messy kisses.

"Congratulations," Stella said, kissing Winston on each cheek. Cate and Andie took turns hugging Emma, as the photographer, a woman in a man's gray suit, knelt down in front of them and snapped a few pictures.

"That is one fabulous-looking family!" she cried. "Now let's have all of you under the archway." She shooed them backward with one hand.

"Yes!" Lola cried, bouncing up and down on her heels. "Our first family picture!"

Stella glanced at Cate, waiting for her to roll her eyes, but she didn't. Emma and Winston beamed. Together, she and Cate struck their best poses for the camera.

Andie turned to Lola. "Ready . . . *sis*?" she asked, a smile creeping over her face.

Lola looked around the garden, at the guests picking appetizers off silver trays. The lead singer of the band had started a more lively song, and one of Winston's Yale friends pulled Greta over to swing dance, spinning her around twice.

"Absolutely," she said, grabbing Andie's arm, and they squeezed in next to their sisters.

EPILOGUE

And they all lived happily ever after. Or not.

The Sloane Sisters maybe be BFFs right now, but at the stroke of midnight, everything can change. After all, it hard to be sisters . . . and even harder to be friends.

And let's be honest—a fairy-tale ending? Where's the fun in that?

ACKNOWLEDGMENTS

First, a huge thank-you to the good people of Alloy Entertainment: The hilarious Josh Bank, a.k.a. Sheila Beers, who has been known to spontaneously channel many of the characters in this series. Sara Shandler, for her sharp editorial insights and, most importantly, for believing. To the fiercely smart Joelle Hobeika, for her enthusiasm, good humor, and reassurance. And to Lanie Davis, for making the connection that started it all.

I'm indebted to Farrin Jacobs and Zareen Jaffery at HarperCollins for their editorial notes and their enthusiasm for this series. A big hug and thank-you to Kate Lee for making my life five thousand times easier.

I'm incredibly fortunate to have such supportive friends, who listened to me and encouraged me every step of this process. Many of them appear in these pages in different incarnations, and this book simply would not have been possible without them. Last but not least, thank you to my brother, Kevin, and my parents, Tom and Elaine, three people who make those words—thank you—seem like a cheap imitation of all the gratitude I feel for them. I love you.